NORTHERN CREATURES

"I'd had more than two centuries of the universe demonstrating to me that even though Victor Frankenstein was more of a monster than I, though he had lied and manipulated, he had—that one time—told the truth...."

FAE TOUCHED

NORTHERN CREATURES BOOK FIVE

KRIS AUSTEN RADCLIFFE

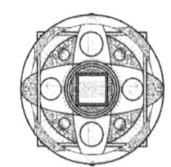

THE WORLDS OF
KRIS AUSTEN RADCLIFFE

Smart Urban Fantasy:

Northern Creatures

Monster Born

Vampire Cursed

Elf Raised

Wolf Hunted

Fae Touched

Death Kissed

God Forsaken

Magic Scorned

Witch Burned (*coming soon*)

Genre-bending Science Fiction about
love, family, and dragons:

WORLD ON FIRE
Series one
Fate Fire Shifter Dragon

Games of Fate

Flux of Skin

Fifth of Blood

Bonds Broken & Silent

All But Human

Men and Beasts

The Burning World

Dragon's Fate and Other Stories

Hot Contemporary Romance:

FAE TOUCHED

NORTHERN CREATURES
Book Five

By
Kris Austen Radcliffe

Six Talon Sign Fantasy & Futuristic Romance
Minneapolis

www.krisaustenradcliffe.com

Published by
Six Talon Sign Fantasy & Futuristic Romance

Edited by Annetta Ribken
Copyedited by Juli Lilly
"Northern Creatures" artwork created by Christina Rausch
Cover to be designed by Covers by Christian
Plus a special thanks to my Proofing Crew.

For requests, please e-mail: publisher@sixtalonsign.com.

First print edition, January 2020
Version: 10.19.2022

ISBN: 978-1-939730-74-9

FAE TOUCHED

CHAPTER 1

It took a full fifty years beyond my rebirth before I was able to pass as a man. Some changes stemmed from elven magic spurring my body to heal. Some happened on their own as my more living parts grew into my more dead. But mostly the changes happened because I left my father behind.

He found a ship after I left him on the Arctic ice, and fed the captain a sad tale of pity and victimhood. Years later, the elves found records. I learned the day before I left to join the Union Army that my father had pinned several murders on me, the son he called vile and monstrous.

I never murdered. Nor was I eight feet tall, or as ugly as he described. All were lies he manufactured as a way to strike at me from beyond his grave.

Those lies were the reason I used the Civil War to test the limits of my invulnerability—and the limits of my personal misanthropy, all of which culminated in my attempted suicide-by-witch.

That moment ended when Rose wrapped her toddler arms around my neck. She didn't believe my father's lies, so for her, I set them aside.

Yet every morning, I was corpse-cold. The elves tattooed over my scars with their beauty, but underneath, my body continued to hitch and halt.

Sally came more for Rose than for me, and I came more for whiskey than for Sally. She said she didn't mind my cold touch, but she did. Then she left.

Benta wanted a wall of misery, and I was happy to oblige.

At one hundred fifty years past my father, I made an effort to live. University reminded me that I was more than my cold flesh. Kindness is its own beauty, and for the first time in my life, women found me acceptable. But Annie was a pixie of a woman, fine-boned and tiny, and I am an ogre of a man. We did not fit together. Not physically. She cried. I cried. And our relationship was no more. Savannah, whom I also loved, tolerated my morning corpse-likeness until I refused to use my intimidating bulk to further her family's automobile dealership fortune. I returned to Alfheim, richer in worldly experience, but poorer of heart.

The eighties and nineties allowed for some easing of my loneliness. I could pass as a professional athlete, and as long as I was warm, I did not lack company.

I still missed Annie. And Sally. And I occasionally wondered what would have happened if my father had not destroyed the female companion he had promised me. We could have commiserated in our ugliness. But instead of a sister, he built a brother more monstrous than I. What if he'd inflicted his horror on a woman? It's best that I am now an only child.

My father told me that I did not deserve someone to ease my suffering. I did not deserve anyone who might listen and offer a touch. I'd had more than two centuries of the universe demonstrating to me that even though Victor Frankenstein was more of a monster than I, though he had lied and manipulated, he had—that one time— told the truth.

Yet some part of me still hoped. Which part, I did not know. The spirits of the men from whom I was molded had long ago entered The Land of the Dead. But something remained. That hope wanted to set aside the self-loathing and the rage. And that hope fell fully, utterly in love.

I am not a fool. Falling in love is simply the discovery of connection. Staying in love is the motion of life. Motion takes work. It takes sacrifice, the kind and quantity of which is determined by the quality of that initial fall. Yet I hope.

When Ellie Jones wrapped her arms around my ice-cold neck, when she cried against my shoulder in the frozen blizzard winds, when she whispered "You're here," that hope blossomed into need. We had common ground in sacrifice, Ellie and I. We had common ground in loneliness. We had each other.

And I would fight every mundane and magical on Earth to keep her safe.

CHAPTER 2

"I remember everything," I said. Every blink and blush when she noticed me noticing her. The pain radiating from the tight, stiff bruise on her leg. Her enjoyment of the spaghetti dinner I made. Her semi-confusion when she told me her cottage had once manifested amongst the kangaroos of Alice Springs. Her willingness to help not only me, but the elves, even though not one knew she existed. The loneliness in her eyes when she said I would forget her each evening.

Every night, the boulder of her world came crashing down into her life. Every morning, she fought to roll it back up the same forgotten hill.

This time, she wasn't alone. I carried her through the snow toward the candles and the warmth of her cottage, and my hound who waited inside.

She shook in my arms.

"You're shivering." I crossed the blizzard-swept yard toward her home. I needed to set her down. I was…

… then my foot crossed the threshold of her cottage's door.

I hadn't seen the magic. How had I missed the magic? But I knew—the blizzard. My focus on Ellie. The distraction of my dog. It was here in silky aurora sheets, the green-red magic of the fae. Of things living and alive and bursting with creation. All that breathed on this world—air, water, fire, or ice—all that walked or swam, flew or fluttered, unfurled and reached for the sky, was here on the surface of the bubble surrounding Ellie's cottage.

And for a flash of a split-second, my most feral moments: I hunted hare under the blinding Arctic sun. The raw heat of my sunburn combined with the biting frost of the northern wind and I was the air. The ice. The crackling gravel under my boots. I drank it in. I gnawed on the land's dry peat. I growled as my semi-corpse body tested the hollow limits of hunger. I reveled in the bone-deep need to howl with the wolves.

Feral magic made of tooth and bone, stem and leaf. Magic that was love and power and sex. It all roiled through me, body and soul.

I shook more violently than Ellie's shivers. My head swam. I swayed through the full balance of nature, its weight and its transitions between seasons of birth and death.

Marcus Aurelius barked. Ellie yelped and clung to my neck as if she gripped a floating log on a stormy sea.

I somehow managed not to trip.

"Are you okay?" she asked.

"I…" Never in my life had I come up against such overwhelming magic. I set her down. "The door…"

I was completely through the bubble. My head now reeled in a post-shock kind of way, not actively adding to the spinning but more slowing down after the initial spin.

"Coming inside never affected Chihiro." We'd come into a small foyer area with a stone floor and a lovely ornate wax-rubbed sideboard. An umbrella stand of woven reeds and vines rested in the corner, and wall-mounted hooks held a couple of coats.

Ellie touched my chest. "We'll figure it out."

I looked down just as she reached to close the door behind us. She stretched around me, still shivering but unwilling to move far enough away to allow the cottage to warm her body, and the neckline of her nightgown swung away from her chest.

The entire gown billowed out in front of her and all that soft pale cotton lifted off her breasts.

I stand just under seven feet tall. I always look down at everyone around me, even the elves. And it wasn't as if I'd never seen breasts before.

My brain locked up. Just for a second. I realized a truth I think I'd understood every evening right before I forgot about her. The same truth I felt in my bones every single time I realized I was battling concealment enchantments: The enchantments reset nothing. All they did was disguise the labels I used to think about my memories. Without those labels, without those *words*, I couldn't find in my own head my focus.

So it brewed unfettered and unchained, unconsidered and primal; much the same way I'd been when I awoke on that table in my father's faraway lab.

But this time, my body wasn't full of pain and rage. This time, I'd walked through a fae portal that was all things *alive*.

I lifted her so high her head almost touched the ceiling and buried my face between her wonderfully soft breasts.

Part of me, the part I trained up after the elves found me—that rational muscle I'd worked and processed and given every psychological tool I found in magical ways and mundane books—yelled *No!* You are huge. You are terrifying. You're ugly and a monster and outside normal and you damned well better make sure that at every step along this journey the woman you're with has an escape route.

I never asked for touch. I always made it clear that I was available if a woman wished to touch me.

But I *needed* Ellie. I—

"Frank." Her voice was husky and vibrant and she kissed my forehead and my cheek as she wrapped herself around ice-cold me as if she was the morning sun come to warm life back into my bones. She pointed into the cottage. "Bed," she said, and…

My hound chose that moment to shake off the snow. Ice flew everywhere, hitting me in the face, bouncing down the neck of Ellie's gown, clinking against the glass of the cottage's big window, even flying so far into the little house it landed as loud pops in the fireplace.

"Marcus Aurelius!" I pulled my face away from the sweet warmth of Ellie's neck. "Do you mind?"

Ellie giggled.

My dog *woofed* as he padded toward the stone hearth, open both front and back, that dominated the main room. On the other side of the hearth, I saw the outline of a bathtub. On this side, a settee and a couple of upholstered chairs had been pushed against the wall to make room for the mattress that took up most of the space in front of the fire.

Ellie shivered. I'd let the fae magic uncork the genie under my rational brain and now the woman I loved was *shaking* because I wasn't making the heat of a living man.

I set her down. "I'm sorry," I said. "I'm cold."

Her mouth opened, then snapped shut. Her eyes narrowed slightly. "You were in the blizzard."

"The fire will help." I reached for her hand but pulled back when I realized what I was doing. "You're shivering."

She looked over her shoulder at the fire. When she looked back at me, her face clearly showed that she was processing all this.

Not that she was confused. Or annoyed. Or even that she was surprised. Only that this was not what she'd expected—or wanted, more likely—and that sorting how to deal with my chilly body was something she now had to do.

"I'm sorry," I said. I always said I was sorry when a woman became fully aware of my lack-of-heat. When it sunk in that it wasn't simply a little chilled flesh in the mornings, or cold fingers after coming in from outside.

This was baked into my bones, though "baked" wasn't the best term. More like freeze-dried.

Her lips thinned. "I'll get towels." She kissed my chin and darted toward the corner that must lead into the bathroom.

I got a quick jab-like impression that the magic wanted me to move away from the door. "What?" I asked. Was the cottage talking to me? Like Sal?

No response.

The whole moment felt odd, and distracted, and full of an embarrassed me. And a cold Ellie. An Ellie who had thought she'd have a warm me with her tonight.

My head—my heart, my body—were reeling.

Our canine emperor circled three times then curled up on a big cushion between the fire and the mattress that took up most of the main room's floor space. Cold leaked through the big window as small, whistling rattles. The wall with the sideboard opened into an arch leading into a kitchen. On the other side of the cottage, to the side of the hearth, a rickety-looking spiral staircase wound up into the shadows.

Ellie's home wasn't all that different than my cabin. Smaller. Less modern, but it did its job.

I pulled off my soaked boots and jacket, and picked my way through the pillows, blankets, cushions, magazines, books, and a wooden chest or two surrounding the mattress.

The fire crackled. I breathed and did my best to calm the lightheadedness caused by the fae magic swimming in my mind.

Maybe I shouldn't fight it, I thought. Or maybe I should. I didn't know. But wasn't that the point of life?

The pile of blankets shimmered in lovely greens and blues as if I'd found the freshest, clearest lake. Several more wooden boxes lined the head of the mattress like an uneven mountain range of painted and carved wonder. A vase of lovely pink roses sat on one, and Ellie's melon-sized camera seer-stone on another.

The mattress, though big for Ellie, wasn't long enough for me.

She reappeared with an armful of thick white towels. "They're warm," she said. "I keep them next to the hearth."

She'd already wrapped one around her shoulders. She'd put on new socks and arm warmers under her nightgown, too. The other towels, she handed to me as she sat next to me.

Warmth radiated off the fabric. Heat crackled from the fire. Yet all I saw was that Ellie still shivered.

I didn't dare touch her again. Not until I could do so without causing harm.

She wrapped one of the fluffy towels around my head. "Does the door look different?"

I glanced over her shoulder. The...

What was I looking at? Something important was there, but not at the same time, as if the concealment enchantments had done to it what it did to my memories each evening. I couldn't put my finger on it.

"Every evening, my concealment enchantments crash against the world. Then they crash against my cottage." She touched my cheek. "I think they're crashing against you." She stroked my face before touching my lips. "They are," she said.

I nodded.

"You're here." Her kiss was as warm as the towel, and as soft. "That's all I care about."

My breath hitched. Two hundred years of living with magicals, of seeing and feeling and surviving, of learning how to be my own rock under the creature sunning itself for warmth...

Not the creature itself. Not the living man.

Ellie looked toward the cottage's door. Her brow furrowed. "Could you wait, please?" she said.

I swear the cottage responded. I swear the sparks of pixie light, of bright yellows and whites and perfect, shimmering pinks that popped in and out of existence on the edges of this place—the edges of my mind—made a memory of a conversation. A node of a past that happened, but didn't happen. I knew about it anyway, as if I was standing on the other side of a veil between one realm and another, experiencing the same time but not the same space.

One side, me in Alfheim; the other, the cottage's fae realm.

It didn't matter which side I was on, as long as I was with Ellie.

Then she pulled me down onto the bed. "The magic's going to make us sleep," she whispered.

Marcus Aurelius sighed. The fire warmed my back and a tingling release moved through my flesh. My beautiful Ellie kissed my cheek.

And I think sleep came even before I closed my eyes.

CHAPTER 3

The magic—or the cottage itself, I couldn't tell which—wanted me to learn, but not in a book kind of way. It wanted me to *understand*, which I did. Or at least I thought I did. I lived with elves. I understood the energy of magic and its patterns and its lights.

Yet I was about to get a lesson in the magical equivalent of quantum field theory.

The scientifically-minded people of the world figured out a long time ago that every "complete" system was actually a node manifested out of the finer grains of another larger, more complex system. Such was how the universe made itself.

Magic was no different.

The elves were part of the universe. They were an important part, a strong part that had coalesced as a self-sustaining magical ecosystem. The elves who had been born of the Nordic pantheon had found a way to become fertile. They birthed babies like their mundanes, but they also wielded the magic of their gods.

There weren't many truly self-sustaining magical groups. The elves. The kami. The fae. Most of the others were spirits that *manifested*. They weren't *born*. They could sometimes make babies like

Akeyla, but they were much more dependent on their mundanes rubbing against the natural world than the elves were.

There were other elf-like magicals out there. Small groups in the Middle East, Africa, India, and in pockets of Oceania. A few still walked the world in South America. Arne once told me the loa were the only group who protected their witches. Rose may have been loa-born, as had the woman I'd faced in my suicide-by-witch attempt in Louisiana.

The power of magic arose from the rubbing of humanity against nature. That rip, that spark, made eddies. And sometimes those eddies, if strong enough, tighten into life magic. Or if those forces happen on the other side of the dominion veil, death magic.

Vampires. Demons. Gods of the dead.

This I knew. This much was as obvious as gravity.

But I'd met *other* magicals.

The fire heated the air inside the cottage. Outside, wind howled and ice pellets bounced against the window. The ice added a high-pitched tinkling to the log's lower crackle in a strange, semi-rhythmic cadence. The world breathed as if startled, in quick icy inhalations and lower, halting pops of warmth.

Ellie, though, breathed slow and steady in her sleep. I did, as well. I dreamed lucidly of this place, and its library—there was a library here, somehow out of sight in a space that was half the size of my own cabin. It was here, real, yet unavailable and unseen until the cottage said so.

I had to learn, first. I had to understand.

The cottage's magic wafted in the fire's updrafts as a thick sturdy column of earthy browns. Blues and greens wavered like the rustling leaves of a tree.

A tree I knew.

The world had other spirits.

Raven was more than the sum of her corvid mythologies. The World Wolf was more than the sum of its weres and its wolves. There were others. A cat. A raptor. A snake and a stag. World spirits of sea, air, and land.

Whoever built Ellie's cottage had called on more than fae magic. She'd pulled on the shadows of the dark forests and beasts that shelter under those limbs. Yet Ellie shimmered like the sun herself.

Why? In my dream state, I did not know. But the cottage did, and she touched the tattoo of Yggdrasil that coiled along the side of my head.

The parts that still burned from St. Martin's magic healed. That pain, at least, left my body. The World Tree gave me this boon.

And I think, in the dream, I understood. It wouldn't matter in the morning. That "understanding" would vanish under a layer of articulation that did not connect the correct words to the concepts I'd just learned.

But it would be there, deep in my sturdy bones and my strong tall limbs. And the World Tree was satisfied.

Marcus Aurelius had always been a polite hound. He never barked to wake me in the mornings. He didn't claw or jump on the bed. My dog laid his head on the mattress next to my pillow, his big puppy snout as close to my face as he could get it, and let out a small, concerned whine.

I always wondered if he thought I was truly dead.

This morning, instead of the whine, he licked my nose. I went from the darkness right at the boundary between the dream world and waking, to a sudden awareness that my dog had needs.

I wasn't in my bed. I wasn't in my house. There'd been an elf and I'd trekked…

I rolled over.

Ellie slept on the other side of the mattress under a mountain of blue and green blankets. Only a little of her skin was visible inside her cocoon of warmth, mostly her cheek, and strands of her auburn hair pooled just under the bone. She sighed, and her eyes twitched. She was sound asleep.

I was in Ellie's bed, in her cottage somewhere in the woods near my lake. In her fae-magicked home. The same place that last night had hit me with fae drunkenness. And a primal, magical dream.

I was supposed to understand something I didn't remember. But of course I wouldn't remember. Fae magic was all about the gut and the limbic system.

Ellie smacked her lips and sighed again.

I was close enough I could thread my hand under that mound of blankets and set it on the roundness of her hip. I could move close and stroke those strands off her cheek and whisper "Good morning." But I was cold.

Ice cold, to the point that I was well aware of my own chill. I'd been out in the snow before I came here and hadn't had time to warm in front of the fire before the cottage knocked me out for its late-night magical light show.

Ellie didn't need to be touched by an iceberg.

I gently rolled toward my dog. He sniffed at my face, then lifted his head as if to look over my shoulder at Ellie.

He couldn't unless he jumped onto the bed. Which didn't make sense, because the mattress was on the floor. Except it wasn't. What had been a mattress was now a bed—a huge bed, one at least three feet longer and wider than it had been last night. The boxes at the head of the mattress were still there, but now they sat in a bookcase-like headboard. The blankets had also grown in size. While we slept, the bed had adjusted to me.

I slowly sat up. The window hadn't changed. It still snowed outside, but the flakes were fewer and farther apart, and the sky lightened. The cloud cover lessened.

The settee that had been pushed to the wall was gone. The two chairs were still there, as was the small table between them, but the big piece of furniture had vanished to make enough room to walk comfortably around the new and improved bed.

The creaky spiral stairs were still around the corner of the hearth, which also hadn't changed. The painting over the fireplace looked different. I couldn't put my finger on how, other than I was pretty sure the colors had moved from reddish to more blues and purples and that the overall pattern of the landscape depicted had somehow shifted.

When I'd come in, the kitchen on the other side of the arch had been dark. I'd gotten a sense of it anyway, of the table and the sink and the counters, and how it filled the other part of the cottage I'd seen from outside. There was a second exterior door in there somewhere, one that led to the part of the yard with the pump. All had seemed correct spatially, and I hadn't paid attention.

The space no longer made sense.

The front door now opened into an added mudroom. A glimpse of the new external wall was just visible through the big window. On the other side of the new room, the kitchen had been greatly expanded. Something warm and golden glowed in there just outside my line of sight.

Ellie sighed in her sleep. My hound wagged his tail as if he expected me to figure out where the magical mystical cottage stored the dog food.

I patted his head. "Hold on," I whispered.

He did a small hound shake, then backed toward the embers in the hearth. I swung my legs off the bed. I was still in my t-shirt and jeans, which was probably for the best. The fabric had likely kept my body from radiating its cold toward Ellie as we slept.

I needed either high-intensity exercise or to stoke the fire. I added two logs, doing my best to be gentle and quiet, then turned toward the kitchen and my hound's quest to be let out, and for food.

He watched me from the arch. I followed him through into what I thought was just a kitchen.

The cottage had added a sunroom during the night. What had been the outside snow-covered area with the pump and the pond was now inside under a passive solar roof. A small waterfall aerated the water, and fish *plimped* at the surface as if they, too, were looking to be fed. A small horde of plants filled in around the pond. Some were tropical, like the big umbrella tree, and others were small harvestable herbs and leafy greens.

And there, in the middle of the big plants, was a pallet with a thick, bed-sized cushion like the one I sat on when sunning myself on my deck.

Marcus Aurelius trotted toward the doggy door carved into the wall next to the back door. "That explains your comings and goings," I muttered. The cottage gave my dog his own door. It also built me a golden-glowing, so warm I felt the heat radiating from the pallet, sunning spot.

Rejuvenation magic swirled around it in soft, slow waves, the kind that recharged and balanced. It was often place-specific and dependent on the ambient energy of the nature around it. The elves had built a few similar places, most of which were inside the magic bubble surrounding The Great Hall.

I had never asked for such a spell to be created along my lakeshore. I wanted to learn to do the calming myself. I would rather it be centered in me than in someone else's magic.

Yet one night inside Ellie's concealment enchantments, and her fae-magical cottage built me this extraordinary gift.

Should I be afraid? I should be afraid. Fae gifts were often not... balanced.

But that was the way of the fae. Either you were all-in, or you were fighting not to drown under the all-in you wished to escape.

I glanced back at the bed, then back at the pallet. I had a choice here. One I wasn't quite sure what to make of, because like all fae-created choices, there was no way it was about the obvious alternatives. This was not about going all-in with Ellie. It wasn't about falling in love with a fae-born witch, or the family-blending work we had coming.

This wasn't about the mundane parts of dating. This was about going all-in with Ellie's magic.

Marcus Aurelius escaped through his doggy door. A puff of cold rolled along the floor, under the kitchen table, and to my feet.

"I live with elves," I said to the cottage. "They're the family that comes with me. This is their land. If I'm going to deal with your magic, you're going to have to deal with them." Was I offering the cottage a deal? *I'm an idiot*, I thought. Never make a deal with the fae.

"Frank?"

I looked back through the arch at the bed just as the mound of blankets exploded.

"Frank?" Ellie shrieked.

I'd been quiet. I'd let her sleep. She didn't know where I was. "I'm in the kitchen!" I should have realized.

I'd panicked my girlfriend.

CHAPTER 4

E llie burst from the bed. "Don't do that!" she shouted.
      I wasn't sure her reaction was about me not waking her, but
it was a pretty good bet. "You were sleeping. I didn't want to wake
you."

Her bottom lip did a real, honest quiver. She bit it and blinked,
then ran through the arch into my arms. "I thought the cottage sent
you home." Her eyes rounded and her lip did that ever-so-tiny wiggle
again. "Or that I'd moved and left you in the snow or… or…"

I was too cold to give comfort. I hugged her close anyway. "I'm
sorry." She curled against my chest. "I didn't realize."

She sniffled. "I thought I'd lost you. I thought my magic rejected
you. I don't want to move again. I…" She trembled.

Was she cold or scared? She was definitely cold. And scared.

"I'm sorry." I had no idea what else to say. "The cottage changed
during the night and distracted me. I didn't think. I'm so sorry." I did
my best to keep my bare skin off hers. She wore her nightgown, and
thick handmade socks and handwarmers, but my forearms and half
my biceps were bare beyond my t-shirt sleeves.

My need for her was tertiary to all this. It had to be. I had to get a
handle on the situation, on the fae promises and the Ellie touches and

the fact that I had no idea how to parse what the cottage wanted or needed. And that I obviously didn't know what Ellie wanted or needed, either.

"Always wake me, or leave a note," she said.

That might not always work, I thought. It might not. But this particular *not* wasn't the point at the moment, even if such pedantic structures often were the point of fae magic.

Again, all-in, or drowning under wave after wave of that all-in.

So I made my choice. I kissed the top of Ellie's head and stroked her back even though I was much too cold. If the fae magic of her cottage was going to mess with me, it was going to mess with me. Like life, magic always found a way. "I will always let you know where I am," I said. At least I had Ellie.

She looked up at my face. "Promise me."

"I promise." I'd just stepped off a cliff. Or into crashing waves. Or into the best thing that has ever happened to me.

Probably all three.

She glanced around my arm. "So that's why the magic knocked us out right away last night." She didn't move away even though I could tell the chill wafting off my chest was beginning to make her tense up. "It does that when it makes changes. I was expecting the bed to upgrade. It's winter. That's why the mattress moved to the fire a couple of nights ago." She pointed over her shoulder. "The cottage made the doggy door for Marcus Aurelius the first night he stayed. It picked up on Chihiro's love of flowers, so there are always roses or cherry blossoms or tulips now, but this..." She waved at the new inside garden. "I think it..." She snapped her mouth shut.

Her lovely blue eyes rounded into big circles and her shoulders tightened. Had she just realized we were all-in here? But I was pretty sure the intelligent woman rapidly blinking at how her cottage had doubled its kitchen footprint knew exactly what was happening.

"What?" Though I might have somehow damaged her magic. An addition took significant spellwork and energy. I frowned.

She placed her hand on my chest. She slowly inhaled but the

tension in her shoulders didn't leave. "You said last night that you remember everything."

"I do." All of it, from the muffin at Lara's to the pike through my chest to all the times she kissed me even though I'd slept with Benta.

Benta. *Damn it*, I thought.

The guilty fear rose up in my chest again. The same *What did I do this time?* response that manifested whenever I messed up. My awareness of that guilty fear coiled around the fear itself, and then another coil added itself—my annoyance that I was once again dealing with the entire rich ecosystem of my unwanted, feared, rage-filled, pained life.

I should have been well beyond this. I *was* beyond it. The elves taught me how to deal with my emotions in a healthy way. I taught myself. I knew what to do.

Breathe. Be calm. Look for a solution. Or be elven and never speak of the past.

None of which were going to work this time.

She stared around my arm at the golden glow and the sweet plinking of the pond. "You told me how you feel. When we were stuck in Vampland. You were on that stupid pike and I think you thought you were going to die so you flat-out told me."

I'd told her I fall in love easily. I feel easily. My father gave me a hitching body, but my emotions? They flowed smoothly to the surface.

"Do you remember when you helped me with the photo Chihiro took? The one of when the cottage moved here?"

I nodded. "I didn't see death." I saw the World Tree.

"I'm a witch, Frank." She looked up at me. "My mother is fae. My father was a mundane man. A talented man who charmed my mother with his music and art, but a mundane nonetheless." She waved her hand in front of herself. "I should be burning up with witch magic."

The mundane part of a witch resisted the magic, and like all resistors, that resistance causes problems—heat, disconnection, sometimes insanity. But not always. Some witches can channel the sparks. Most couldn't. Rose burned up from her witch magic. It ate her body and soul and she ended her life in a fire so hot Alfheim's magic couldn't stop it.

The spellwork of the cottage probably drained the magic away at night, when it closed up. It seemed the most likely—and the best way —to harness her power. It was also the likely reason neither Ellie nor the cottage brimmed with visible magic while it was open. All the work was done at night, while she fed the battery.

She stared at the pallet and the big, fluffy cushion. "*I* fuel this place," she said. "*I* fuel my seer stone. It all comes down to me."

"You're the battery that drives the spells." All the intricacy here, the level of harnessed magic—the entire system was in place to drain off Ellie's natural witch overheating. The concealments, the ability to move to different locations, the reconfiguring all used up the substantial power she must produce.

A warm breeze moved through the plants. Ellie inhaled again and blinked, as if steadying herself to walk off her own cliff. "*That is my* lack of poker face." She pointed at the new addition.

I frowned again. I wasn't quite sure what—

She looked up at me with the most open and trusting face that any woman ever had in my two hundred years. The most frightened, too. And the most vulnerable.

And nothing else mattered. Not my fear concerning Benta. Not the cottage's magic, or my lack of understanding. Only Ellie.

She yanked at my t-shirt. I grabbed her hands but she splayed her fingers over my abdomen. I could only bring ice to this particular table. "I'm cold."

Warmth flowed from her palms to my flesh and I sighed.

She touched me and my body melted under her hands and I didn't think it was her magic. It was her. I warmed because of Ellie.

It should be the other way. I was big and muscular and I should be the heat source on which she sunned, not the other way around.

"Does it hurt?" she asked.

"Does what hurt?" My entire body ached. Every major muscle group—my shoulders, lower back, hamstrings, biceps and triceps, even my ankles—always argued and complained when I was cold. I was tight but not consistently across my whole body, which caused yanking in some parts, and bunching in others. The clamminess caused the firing of nerves meant to draw attention to when a body was outside its normal homeostasis range, that "we're edging toward danger" borderline flu-like dullness signaling a need to recuperate.

Such were my mornings, every morning. Every day. All the time, if I wanted to admit it. The pain was a background reminder that I was reconstituted.

Ellie pushed my t-shirt higher as she moved closer. "When you're cold? It hurts, doesn't it?" She placed her cheek over my heart and wrapped her arms around my waist.

"Yes." I wouldn't lie.

She pressed against my front. "Let me help," she whispered.

I don't quake. But I am human, and some anticipation, some excitement, found its way to my muscles. All the feral energy from the previous night roared back. All those desires and the wants that I long ago leashed because no woman wanted a corpse in her bed.

Yet Ellie did. She did. That's what she meant by her own lack of poker face. I could read her emotions from her magic as well as she could read mine on my face.

She wanted me, and not just because she wanted protection inside my big, frightening bubble. Or because we hated ourselves in parallel. She wanted me because I'd put in the work and found my way to her through blizzards and concealments.

I had to trust that she was going to put in the work, too.

A part of me, a small annoying part, screamed like a terrified raccoon cornered against a shed. What if she got sick of the work? What if this tolerance of my corpse-like flesh had an expiration date? Then I would be all-in with disgusted fae magic.

That raccoon wanted to return to being lost in the woods so it didn't have to deal with the inevitable, and it would bite any hand that offered food, or comfort, or understanding.

I pressed my lips against the top of her head anyway.

Ellie stepped back. She pulled her nightgown up and over her head.

My girlfriend stood in front of me naked, except for her over-the-knee hand-knitted socks and her over-the-elbow hand-knitted arm warmers.

Every bit of my overthinking shut down. That raccoon suddenly decided that some things are worth sticking around for. I decided—my body decided—that this once, I should shut up and allow Ellie to define the moment.

It probably wasn't the smartest thing I've ever done. Or maybe it was.

She grasped the warmer on her left arm to pull it off.

"Leave it on." The words rumbled out of my chest.

The most beautiful, happy, wonderful smile she'd yet given me shone as bright on her face as the golden glow shimmered on the plants behind us. I scooped her up. The magic and its manipulations be damned. My cold flesh, too.

Time for me to dive over that cliff, that damned raccoon head-locked under my arm, into the most terrifying waves of my two hundred years.

Hopefully, none of us would drown.

CHAPTER 5

The sky outside had brightened—we had to be past noon—and the clouds had moved beyond their blizzard roiling and into smooth and steady. Light snow drifted down toward the skylight directly over my sunning cushion but somehow didn't accumulate. The skylight also filtered the light, warming it more than it should under an overcast, winter sky, which benefited not only me, but also my hound, the plants, and I assumed the fish in the pond.

The magic of Ellie's space had been thorough when building the sunroom. It wrapped us in a cocoon of feminine comfort of soft round pillows and gentle embraces. It melted my body's stress. It gave us a nest.

I dozed in the warmth, sprawled on the bed-sized cushion under a sweet-scented, ultra-soft blanket, with Ellie sprawled on top of me—fully on top of me, with her arms around my chest and legs curled around mine. She breathed against my shoulder. Her auburn hair tickled my neck. For the first time in my life, a woman chose not to break contact after intimacy.

I could stay like this forever, warm and with her. Calmed by her weight and the rhythms of her body. My beautiful, perfect Ellie.

She snoozed and part of me was sure I was going to end up paying for this bliss.

Marcus Aurelius slept on an equally cushy doggy bed between a seven-foot Schefflera tree and a table brimming with edible greens. The snow was letting up. Ellie shimmered in the golden sunshine. The world righted against the attacks on Alfheim. Yet I couldn't get past the thought that on the scales of the universe the totality of my life didn't balance with this moment.

No one, no matter how good or brilliant or strong, was worthy of the love of a woman like Ellie.

Her breath tickled the crook of my neck. *"Hmm…"* She slid her hand over my hip. "You're warm now."

I chuckled.

She kissed my neck and ran her hand up my side to my chest. "I'm going to take more photos of you," she said in a husky hungry voice.

The look in her eyes said she was serious.

This is new, I thought, though it wasn't surprising. We had no problem fitting together physically, which had made her as happy as it made me. Gleeful, honestly, and enthusiastic.

The part where a woman wanted photos of me was new. Since the eighties, the novelty of my height and build had made me as attractive as it had terrifying. It was nice, I supposed, to be the human equivalent of a roller coaster—scary yet too entertaining to pass up.

Ellie traced her finger along the scar across my right pec. "I'm going to find every tight muscle and every tissue pull and I'm going to fix them for you."

Did I want to be a project? "That's a lot of work," I said.

She blinked. Her mouth rounded. "I'm half fae, Frank." She said it as if her meaning was as clear as the sweet, bell-like tinkling from the plants around us.

And there it was, the all-in nature of the fae.

Ellie frowned.

What had Arne said about his fae princess? The woman he knew long ago before he came to the New World? The one who, even though elves did not speak of the past, had made enough of an impact on his life that he was willing to speak of her now?

She was all things feminine, son. You can't fight that.

I was in love with a fae-born seer. We were on this rollercoaster together. I might as well sit back and enjoy the ride.

"What happened to your father?"

She returned her head to my shoulder. "He's dead. A mundane disease took him."

"I'm sorry."

"My mother won't hurt you," she said.

New, screamed through the back of my brain. But what the hell was I expecting? I should probably throw my hands in the air and hoot as we rolled through this particular corkscrew.

Ellie grinned. "Frank, you've figured out who my mom is, right?" She waved her hand at the plants. "This isn't some nymph's work." She kissed my shoulder. "The cottage and the concealments are a lot of effort for a random witch."

Yes, they were.

"My mom's never been all that open as to why the cottage moves, or why I have to deal with the concealments." She snuggled in again. "She's hiding me, obviously." She shrugged. "Though I honestly think she wanted to make sure that anyone who got close to me was worthy."

Worthy. I reflexively hugged her.

She tapped my chest. "You have *nothing* to worry about."

I chuckled even though I needed to get a handle on what was happening here, magic-wise.

"I've long suspected she's hiding me from her husband. I've never met him. He's an ass."

There were a lot of high-born fae. They varied in how they interacted with mundanes and with other magicals. The most powerful had their own realms, pockets like the elven space around The Great Hall, but with the fae, those realms were kingdoms.

The magical tooled-leather exterior of the portfolio Ellie used to carry her photographs represented one such realm. Her camera came from one, as well. So I'd always known she was high-born.

I shouldn't tense. I shouldn't let real fear creep in, either. The fae were just another group of magicals. I could handle magicals.

But I needed to know, just in case. "Who's your stepfather?"

Ellie looked away. "He's not part of my life."

If he knew about her, he was part of her life. "Okay," I said.

She sat up. "He won't bother you. Or the elves. He's not stupid."

The evasion of the question wasn't helping my anxiety.

Ellie sighed and looked up at the skylight. "I'm a princess," she said. "Like a daughter-of-royalty type princess."

I stroked her thigh. "I figured as much." My girlfriend was a stunningly beautiful fae princess with a terrifying family. *You can't fight that*, Arne had said.

She watched me intently for a moment as if trying to figure out what all-in meant from the fae side of the magicks. Then she sighed again.

"My mother is the Queen of the Fae," she said.

"Which one?" There were several Fae Queens in the same way there were several Elven Queens. We had Dag. The other enclaves had their own.

"Frank." She leaned closer. "My mom is *the* Queen of the Fae."

"Like Dag's father is the Elven Emperor?" I asked.

She nodded. "It's not quite the same." Her eyebrows crunched together. "It is, though. The same. Everyone's autonomous unless they do something that might put all the fae at risk. Then Mom steps in. I mean, would you like to spend your days micromanaging goblins and brownies? Mom and her husband don't even interfere with each other."

"Who are they?" I asked softly. She clearly wanted to tell me.

She looked toward my—our—hound. "Emperors are a pain in the ass. Except the puppy kind."

Marcus Aurelius responded with his own soft, sleepy *woof*.

I continued to stroke her thigh. Should I start guessing? Her mother was *the* Queen, and she hedged. I had a few guesses, and none of them were simple, "Hello, dear fae friend! Welcome to Alfheim!" kind of situations.

Ellie looked up at the clearing sky on the other side of the skylight. "My stepfather is Oberon."

I sat up. "*Oberon?*" It'd take more than one Elven Court to protect Alfheim from Oberon, if he decided to come looking for his wife's wayward child.

Which meant Ellie Jones was the witch-daughter of the most problematic fae on Earth. "Your mother is Titania," I said.

She nodded. "Yes."

Her mother wasn't problematic because of her magical power level, though it was substantial. She was problematic because of all the fae, Titania—and Oberon—were the best-known and most beloved by mundanes. And if I'd learned anything from Arne and Dag, it was that magicals with mundane buy-in were forces to be reckoned with.

"We need to tell the elves," I said.

Ellie placed both her hands on my chest. "This is why I didn't say anything right away."

I wasn't blaming her for not telling me the moment we met. "I don't talk about my father unless I'm asked," I said.

She looked away again. "Yes, you do. You told me about him, and your past, when we had our one date. You make sure there's no secrets. You're a good man."

The night I made her dinner. "You told me about where your cottage has been." And that she was fae-born. She'd given me the information she felt comfortable giving. No harm in that.

"I'm sorry." She wiped at her eye. "It's just that..." She sniffed. "I landed in elf territory. What if they'd figured out they had Titania's daughter in their midst? Even with the concealments, their magic is strong. If you knew, you wouldn't have done what you're doing now. Being good. My mother's presence eclipses everything. And if there's a threat..."

A threat would have spurred the cottage to move again. "We'll be careful," I said. "I'll mediate if I have to. Arne and Dag won't hurt you once they know. They're good with outsiders."

"I think they know." Ellie chuckled. "At first, I thought your Queen was a Heimdall aspect and that she somehow heard me chewing my toast or humming in the yard through the concealments. Then I realized what was happening."

Arne and Dag knew about Ellie? "Dag hasn't taken an aspect name." Most elves with her power level owned up to their god aspect. Most of the ones who didn't were women, though.

Ellie leaned closer. "That's because there's not supposed to be more than one All-Parent per enclave. Such concentrations of power tend to lead to a disruption in elven hierarchies. Sort of like when that playwright decided to openly name a character after my mother." She flared her fingers. "Boom! A cataclysmic shift in power."

Dagrun Tyrsdottir was an All-Parent? "Dag's another aspect of Odin?"

Ellie nodded. "She wields more power than the King."

"We have two Odin aspects in Alfheim?" We have two Thor elves. Magnus wasn't our only Freyr elf, either, though the other Freyrsson was less powerful and thus able to control his effects on mundanes. We also had our own Bragi, and a Saga, both of whom taught at the high school. And I'd long wondered if Sif the Golden was in fact an aspect of Sif, and if Benta was an aspect of Freya.

But two Odins? "And here I thought Dag was probably a Friggsdottir."

Ellie reached for her socks. "That's Sif the Golden."

"You know all this?" She knew more about the elves than I did, and I'd lived with them for two centuries. I reached for my own clothes.

"I know the god aspects of all the elves I've photographed." She grinned and kissed my cheek. "I know yours, too."

I stopped half bent over the edge of the cushion as I reached for my pants. "What?" I was mundane. I didn't have an aspect. The jotunn thing was a joke.

The next kiss landed on my hip, since I'd leaned away. "You're my own personal Baldur," she purred.

I blinked.

She pouted. "You *cannot* take a compliment, can you, Mister Serious?"

Ellie, still naked except for one thigh-high sock, batted her eyelashes like she didn't want us to get dressed.

Had she just sprung a trap? Because I was caught. I'd been caught down at the lakeside, that first day. I followed my dear dog and we both crawled right into that box because we knew a damned good thing when we saw it. How many fires had Ellie jumped into for us? How much damage had she taken? I'd found a good person. A good soul.

Ellie tangled her arms around my head. Her soft breasts pressed against my chest. I wrapped my arms around her bare back and stroked her shoulders with my sun-warmed palms.

She kissed me deeply. "I love your lack of poker face."

I hadn't told her how I felt. I had, but not since I passed through the concealment enchantments. Not since I acknowledged that I was all-in.

Why did I keep waffling like I didn't know what all-in meant? Like my lungs suddenly thought I was drowning on dry land? Because I'd fought for this. I followed Chihiro's directions and I took notes and I did everything I could to remember Ellie. I trudged through a blizzard on the off chance an odd elf had actually given me good advice. All because I was in love.

"We will get this sorted," I said. "And stabilized."

"*Hmmm…*" She kissed me again. "Make me happy first."

Yes, this was what I'd fought for. This was what I'd wanted even before I left my father on that ice floe. A partner who wanted me—all of me—no matter how I lumbered through this world.

Ellie giggled when I flipped her onto the cushion. "We're going to need to go back to my place, you know." I nibbled on her neck, which elicited a sigh. "My perfect, time-stealing fae princess."

This was what Arne meant when he said *you can't fight that*. One can't fight the arms of a fae who freely gave her attentions. And no matter the rollercoasters, or waves, or whatever, I'd be a fool if I tried.

CHAPTER 6

The winter slapped us in the face the moment we stepped outside. Low flat gray clouds, the kind that don't break up so much as stop being when they run out of snow, still drifted over Alfheim. Not a lot of new flakes fell. The wind, though, had picked up again and continued howling as if Fenrir himself had slipped his bonds.

Ellie swore as she pulled her hat lower over her ears. "How do you live here?"

Once Ellie and I stepped through the cottage's gate, I knew exactly where her cottage was in relation to my cabin, the lake, and the road. All this time, Ellie had been nestled into a stand of birch and cedar less than a quarter mile from my home, on a small rise in the dead center of the peninsula that separated my place from most of the new lots.

I came this way almost every time I went out to look for Marcus Aurelius. I'd walked by her gate at least thirty times.

My hound bounded happily by, obviously more excited about the snow than Ellie. His favorite humans were heading back to his primary living space. What else could a dog want?

"It's not so bad," I said. "Marcus Aurelius likes it. Could be worse.

Snow won't stay anyway. It'll melt by tomorrow afternoon." Samhain was too early for sustained snow cover these days. When I first walked into Alfheim, it wasn't. But now? Mundanes were destructive to the natural world.

Ellie stopped trudging through the wet, deep snow and shook her foot. "I need new boots."

"We'll go into town. Roads should be clear by now." Nothing Bloodyhood's new plow couldn't scrape off the driveway anyway.

I needed to check in with the elves and figure out some way to let them know about Titania. Maybe. On one hand, they should know, but on the other, with the concealments, "knowing" might end up being more panic than contemplation.

Unless I figured out how to permanently break the enchantments.

Ellie asked a continuous stream of questions about how best to outfit her and the cottage for a Minnesota winter. "I wonder if the cottage would allow solar panels?" She looked over her shoulder. "I'd like a laptop." She gripped my arm as we moved around snow-heaped bushes. "And a regular camera. A DSLR. And a warmer jacket." She hitched the strap of her backpack up her shoulder.

Mostly, though, all the little domestic desires and all the small changes felt needed, but not needed in a way that was being forced on me as a time-consuming to do list. She trusted me to pick out a camera, and to figure out how to wire her cottage to take solar panels.

Before any shopping, we needed to make sure Arne had taken care of Dag. She'd been injured when I left and was probably getting yet another cast on her wrist at the clinic right now. Then there was the question of the *other* elf, the one who'd helped me find Ellie. I couldn't remember how he looked, beyond a strong sense of *different*. I couldn't remember his name, either, even though I was sure he'd told me.

He'd helped the kids, too. Protected them, somehow. If only my brain would bother to remember.

Perhaps Ellie's concealments were still messing with my head. Either way, my gut said to tread lightly with the unknown elf.

She squeezed my hand through our gloves. "I follow this path every time I go to your place. Now that the cottage has accepted you, you'll be able to find your way back with no problems."

There'd be issues, of course. Would the cottage let me bring a ladder down the path? The roof near the chimney needed a looking-at before we started thinking about solar panels. Could I bring Sal? Ed? No elves, obviously. Where was the actual edge of what the concealment enchantments would allow? And was there a way to make sure the cottage truly anchored here? I didn't want to accidently scare it and cause a move.

The storm remnant still fritzing at Alfheim suddenly coiled down the sides of my neck, under my jacket, and to my chest. I'd been so focused on the all-in nature of fae magic that I hadn't thought about the possibility that it might get miffed and do something passive-aggressive the first time I wasn't able to spend the night.

Or fold me into the enchantments so all of Alfheim forgot me, too.

What was I getting myself into? I'd find out soon enough.

Ellie ran her hand over the trunk of one of the two big oaks that acted as a semi-gate between my property and the wooded area of the peninsula. "The other girl, Akeyla's friend, Sophia, right?"

My phone chimed. We were far enough away from the cottage's orbit I could check my messages. "Ed's daughter." I pulled out my phone.

"She's touched."

Which was pretty obvious from what happened when the kids showed up with Sal. "She remembered you. Jax didn't. Akeyla, neither."

Six messages, two from Arne, one from Maura, one from Remy, and two from Bjorn.

Ellie nodded. "It's not a clean touch," she said. "Not a direct descent from a hero kind-of-thing with one specific god. I swear there's more than one kind of magic mingling in her blood. Like she's an actual, honest-to-all-the-pantheons melting pot."

All the kids were. The whole town was, even if no one here really thought about it, or cared. A lot of the mundanes would get mad, too, if you disparaged the purity of their Scandinavian heritage. Here, the elves were elves, the mundanes were good Norwegian Minnesotans, and kids these days were as confusing as the weather.

I held out my phone. "Looks like I should call in."

Ellie nodded. "I need to take more photos," she said.

My old backpack, the one with the stain on the pocket, had become Ellie's favorite camera and portfolio carrying bag. I doubted she'd give it back. Not that I'd ask. Next she'd be stealing my t-shirts to wear as nightgowns. Which I wouldn't mind. I'd never had a woman borrow my clothes before.

When I realized Ellie was watching me ponder losing my clothes, she smiled and squeezed my hand again.

A beam of sunlight pushed through the clouds and a snowflake caught the light. I instinctively turned toward the little glint, but it was gone before I could make sense of it. "Dancing snow," I said and pointed.

A second glint burst on and off just off my cheek, more like a firefly than crystalline water, then a third, and a fourth, and a fifth in the shadows of the trees.

The lights popped on and off like fireflies, and so quickly I wasn't getting a strong sense of magic around them. They had to be magical. The storm should have killed all the insects and sunlight could only catch so many flakes.

And the only thing I could think of capable of causing twinkling in Alfheim's air was uncontained low-demons like the ones Dracula used. Low-demons the elves eradicated.

Ellie stopped walking. "Frank..." she said as she stepped in front of me.

I pulled her close to my side. "My cabin is on the other side of the trees." The side of the house and the path's access to the deck were no more than fifty feet ahead. But we had deep snow to deal with, and running wasn't really possible.

"Marcus Aurelius! Go!" If Maura was home, he'd bring her down the path. "Bring Maura!"

My dog barked once and ran for the cabin.

"I don't think we're dealing with low-demons," Ellie said.

What else could they be? Enchanted gnats?

One of the flickering points of light manifested directly in front of my face, then flitted to the side to give me a clear view of the snow-covered brambles and low-hanging tree limbs between us and my home.

Two willowy figures stood on each side of a large red oak tree. They were fae, but not just any fae.

We had dryads in full armor between us and my cabin.

CHAPTER 7

R ed oaks don't shed their leaves in the fall, and this particular tree held onto its hand-sized leaves in abundance. Each one had curled and dried to a warm, leather-like bronze that rustled in the winter wind. Those leaves sheltered many a small critter.

The oak towered over the path as one of the brilliantly grand guardians surrounding my home and lake.

The two fae standing on either side of its trunk carried the same sturdy, tall strength. Their armor shimmered with the white of the snow and the gray-blue of the sky even as it carried the roughness of the tree's bark. The rough surface coiled down the plating over their thighs, onto the worked leather of their boots, and into the snowpack as if the fae were as rooted to the ground as the oak.

Their helmets shadowed blue-rimmed eyes and carried magnificent racks of antlers textured more like the leather-ish winter oak leaves than anything produced by a stag. Their magic danced close to their bodies like snow blowing in the wind. It hid their true heights and gave me the sense that the two bodies in front of us might well have been optical illusions created to trick our senses.

The fae were objects at a distance reflected oddly in reality's mirror.

These were not simple dryads. Nymphs were female but these two melded the duality of male and female into a steadfast singularity. They also carried the magic of an oak's animals—the deer, the jay around their eyes, the squirrel in the softness of tunics under their armor—which regular dryads did not.

"Can they see us?" I asked. Ellie's concealments hid her from magicals but I had no idea if they worked on other fae.

She backed toward me. "My concealments work on other fae. I think it's to keep my stepfather or his minions from finding me." She spoke in a way that made me think she wasn't so sure of her answer.

The dryads' armor radiated *in service of the high-born* but not which high-born King or Queen. Not that I had enough experience—any experience, honestly—with fae to be able to read anything beyond the presence of their magic. The only fae other than Ellie I'd ever been near was the one disturbed by the Civil War. He'd been a fae of the valley, probably a type of Green Man, and not in service of royalty.

Samhain chaos drew them to this land. They'd come to learn from the trees.

I blinked. How...

I *knew* they were here to question the forest in much the same way I knew what Sal wanted me to know, but this seemed more like a broadcast than a statement.

Ellie gripped my hand and looked up at my face. "Did you hear that? They're here to speak to the trees?"

"Sal talks to me the same way." I nodded toward the forest. Which made some sense, since I was pretty sure they were some type of warrior dryad. "They're here for this place, not us."

I hoped. Me breaking Ellie's enchantments was very much a part of last night's magical blizzard.

Ah, Ellie mouthed, and nodded twice. She twisted in such a way to keep her backpack next to my side and out of the possible line of fire.

I'd seen mentions of lieutenants who managed a royal's mundane interactions, and of how one should never underestimate the mercurial nature of the fae. But never dryad warriors who came to speak to the trees.

The two fae held perfectly still like two statues built from winter itself.

And I knew more: Veils were pierced under the Samhain moon. Mingling occurred. The wind shrieked and lightning illuminated what hid in shadows. They'd come to gather acorns of truth.

I understood *under* language, in memory-thoughts, as if the two dryads were giving the world information and not me.

"What does that mean?" Ellie asked.

The two fae spread their arms and… the world flowed *toward* them as if reality itself was whispering secrets to its closest confidants.

Secrets about the slime left by St. Martin's footsteps through these woods. Tales of magicals as they traveled between the winds of the blizzard. Recountings of magicks worked. Of the determination and anger of elves and the bright, quick wolfness of Axlam and the Pack.

Of the steadfast one who had found his way to this land.

Me, I thought.

"The land is telling them about last night." The memory-thoughts were clearly linked to the web of magic set up by the elves, and followed a stream flowing from the past into the present.

The two fae abruptly pulled in their hands. Power shifted, or more precisely, *sifted*.

"They're looking for something," I said. Or someone.

Ellie curled her arm around my waist.

I instinctively pulled her close even though I hadn't gotten a sense that the two armored-up dryads were looking for her.

But that undercurrent had returned. The fae river of below-language knowledge. And deep inside, I knew all non-fae information they gathered was just that—information.

Except… There should not be fae magic here. Not where it could be subsumed by elves, or wolves, or the thin vampire residue remaining around Alfheim.

This knowledge caused surprise and wrath combined.

Ellie inhaled as if she swallowed a gasp. "They shouldn't sense the concealments."

We had fae bloodhounds sniffing around—bloodhounds who

came here specifically because the land rang out with fae magic. Bloodhounds who could very well be from Oberon's Court.

"It might not be you." How could it *not* be Ellie?

It could be me.

I broke through the concealments. I caused Ellie's cottage to reconfigure—profoundly, too, and in a way it never had before. I was at the center of last night's magical St. Martin-generated whirlwinds and I interacted with that strange, black-eyed elf who I barely remembered, as if my brain couldn't be bothered to see him as worth recognizing.

"I'm going to step away from you," I said.

"Oh *no* you are *not*, Frank Victorsson." Ellie pointed at the two dryads as if she'd read my mind as easily as she understood the intent of the dryads. "I'm not losing you to two Cernunnos wannabes."

I'd spent one night in her cottage. One. And here we were with karmic fae coming to make me pay for the bliss of the morning.

"Frank."

I looked down at Ellie. She hitched up the strap of her backpack. Her lips wiggled and bunched and I swear she sniffed because she had tears for the same reason I had cosmic-level doubts: No matter how we fight, or live, or work at building something worthwhile, we were two people who the war dogs always find.

Trials and tests. Clashes and concealments. She and I would always have a fight on our hands.

I twisted my head, listening to the background hum of the two dryads. "I'm going to ask questions." I needed to know why they were surprised and wrathful.

She frowned. "Are you sure about this?"

"I'm not losing *you* to two Cernunnos wannabees." Not after what we went through to find each other. Not after her touching my cold body and asking me if I hurt. Not after a full morning of the most intimate and perfect lovemaking of my two hundred years. I'd throw punches at the King of the Fae himself if I needed to.

Her lips rounded and she blinked. "Okay." She inhaled. "Okay." She shook her arms like she was warming up for a fight. "Be careful."

39

I squeezed her hand, then took two big steps away toward the dryads.

The closer I got, the taller they grew—and the more androgynous. They cocked their heads in mirror image to one another and a memory-thought of me manifesting filled the small clearing—and the knowledge that I was not a creature that should be able to manifest.

"My name is Frank Victorsson," I said. Maybe if I ignored me appearing out of thin air, Ellie's concealments would force the strangeness of it to pass. "This is my lake." I pointed toward my cabin.

Yes. They read me from the land. I was not a creature who manifested.

So much for using Ellie's concealments to my advantage.

Behind me, Ellie removed her pack and unzipped the main pocket.

The air around the fae swirled with ice and took on the clarity of Arctic cold. Neither moved but the balance of friend and foe shifted into *threatening*.

They sensed seer magic.

Ellie lifted her hand off the pack.

I raised my hands. "Sorry!" I said. "I see magic and sometimes magicals sense it as seer magic!" I lied. Anything to keep them off Ellie's scent. Maybe the misdirection would stop the questions about manifesting.

"Do they believe you?" Ellie asked.

"I don't know," I paused, then continued for the two fae, "who you are." Other than the sense of *threat* receding, I picked up no other information.

Ellie zipped the bag and shouldered it again.

I slowly pointed to the elven tattoos around my ear. "This is elf territory. The elves here would not allow calamity to befall the land." Annoyance, yes. But harm? No. "Do you wish to speak to our King and Queen?"

A new wave of knowledge rolled from the dryads: Salt was poured and the truth dusted. There was fae magic here. I was to tell them all I knew.

I rubbed at the top of my head. "We had a wolf problem, but the elves dealt with it last night," I said.

A wave of *seeking* rolled from them. The elves have offended.

This wasn't about my interactions with Ellie's concealments. "How?" I asked. "Why are you here?" I asked.

Reality flickered around the two fae. They were there, then not, then back again but *different*. They'd flipped how they were presented —not just exchanging positions, but flipping what had been on their left to their right as if we were no longer looking at the two fae, but a mirror image.

I'd never seen a magical do anything even remotely similar to the illusions cast by the two fae. Magic was of the world, of the ground under our feet and of the bodies of the creatures working the spells. It was, in essence, more real than the mundane reality around it, and always felt as such. But this, with the mirroring, and the in-the-head echoing, was otherworldly in ways that made every hair on the back of my neck stand on end.

"The elves never do anything that weird," I said.

Ellie's nervous chuckle came out as a high-pitched sneeze. "The fae are nothing if not theatrical."

Theatrics had a purpose: Slight-of-hand saved magical energy. It acted as another layer of camouflage against the mundane world. It twisted and it gave cover.

It wasn't a method the elves used. Norse practicality dictated a sincerity to the elves' lives that made trickery and theatrics distasteful.

The magic swirling around my big red oak obscured and obfuscated. It put on airs and it puffed up.

Like a trickster.

The thought hit me in the same way that I knew what they wanted me to know. It hit like Sal. It smacked me upside the head as if the universe wanted me to pay attention. *Trickster* broadsided me like a truck and I wanted to yank Ellie against my chest as if to protect her from an incoming hit.

She was too far away. "What do you know?" I yelled at the two dryads as if threatening two fae would be enough to stop whatever was coming for us.

They looked to the side, as if someone or something in the trees had caught their attention. Then they looked at each other.

Reality blinked. They vanished.

Ellie exhaled as if she'd been holding her breath. "What happened?"

"Tricksters," I muttered. I immediately returned to her side. "They tossed out *trickster* the same way they tossed out all their poetry."

I scanned the trees looking for any telltale signs of abnormal magic. Nothing. No fae. No elves or wolves or tricksters. Only that word nagging at the inside of my skull.

I'd had my fill of lies and illusions. Of threats. Of powers dark and light deciding I was nothing more than a toy in their grand playpen. Of parents, All- or Royal or hubris-laden, so bound by their own fears that they paid no heed to the reality they manufactured. "Leave Ellie alone," I rumbled. *Leave me alone.*

Let us live.

"Frank…" Ellie rubbed my hand. "You're clenching your fists."

"What?" I looked down at my hand just as I became aware of how deeply into my palm I was digging my fingers.

Not again, I thought. It was an amorphous *not again*, a blob of response formed from the many layers of gummy regrets left behind by so much of my life. Some of those layers had been caused by low-demons. Some by witchly interference. But not all of them.

"Hey hey *hey*…" Ellie cupped my cheeks. "You haven't dealt with fae before? Other than me?"

Only the aftermath of a fae angry about the World Scars caused by the Civil War.

I shook my head.

"Okay." She quickly kissed my lips. "Okay." She pulled her backpack around again. "Those well-versed in fae spellwork leave a wake that can… stir a soul… when they return to their home realms." She squeezed my hand. "They must have been well-versed."

I nodded.

She set her bag on the tops of her feet. "We need to figure out who sent them."

I nodded again.

"Hey." She put her hand on the side of my neck. "Your heart is racing."

It was. I inhaled deeply as I attempted to calm myself.

"No fae showed up when Chihiro got through my concealments."

This still might be my interactions with her cottage. We didn't know. Whatever it was about, it definitely affected *me*.

Ellie stopped digging in her bag long enough to give me a quick hug. She didn't say anything else, but she watched me closely as if trying to figure out if I was okay. "Do you still feel strange? Is it coming from any particular direction?" She pulled out her camera and held it up as if to ask what she should photograph first.

No admonishments for my moment of overreacting. No shrinking away in fear. She trusted me to get through this.

I love this woman, I thought, as if I hadn't fully accepted the possibility until now.

"Now that they're gone, I'm taking pictures," she said.

The fae better not mess up the best thing that ever happened to me. I nodded again, whipped out my phone, and dialed the one elf who might have answers.

CHAPTER 8

W e found Marcus Aurelius waiting by the patio door. He cowered a little as if the two dryads had frightened him, and leaned against the glass.

No one was home to let him in. I rubbed his head again and tried calling Arne one more time.

He didn't answer. I left him a message not unlike the two he'd left me—please call as soon as possible. Maura hadn't answered, either. Nor had Bjorn. I left multiple messages. "Odd," I said, and tucked away my phone.

Ellie stomped her feet and followed my dog through the door. She'd taken six photos, and had tucked the plates into her portfolio to await developing back at the cottage.

Neither of us expected much of the images. The two dryads left no residual magic I could see, and Ellie felt nothing. But still, we needed to try.

"Hello?" I called, just in case. Maura not being home was strange, since Akeyla should be arriving home from school about now.

Ellie rummaged through the mail and papers on the kitchen table. "A note." She held up a bright pink piece of paper. "They're going straight to the hospital after school." She paused. "You're supposed to call Arne."

Which I already knew. "Hospital?" I took the paper and there, along the bottom in Maura's elegant hand, was *Mom needed to stay overnight.*

"How bad were her injuries?" Ellie asked.

I stared at the words. "She told me to leave," I said. "She hid how badly she'd been hurt." Why would I have expected The Elf Queen of Alfheim to show me her real pain?

If I'd known, I would have carried Dag out, too.

Ellie gripped my arm. "You got Axlam to safety. You did as Queen Dagrun asked."

But I didn't go back. I might have saved Dag some of the severity of her injuries. But if I had, I wouldn't be standing here fully aware of my history with Ellie. I wouldn't have spent the night. And I wondered if we would have gotten a dryad visitation if I'd helped the woman I considered my mother instead of finding the woman I loved.

Ellie walked around the table and touched my hand so I'd put down the note. "Pack a bag. Get Sal. We'll go to the hospital then home to develop the photos."

I hugged her against my side. What was done was done. All I could do now was to offer the elves help and information. "Okay."

I wrote my own note, fed my dog, and gathered my things while Ellie rummaged through the hall closet trying on Maura's random winter coats and boots. We'd go shopping, but Maura wouldn't miss a scarf or two in the meantime.

I set a bag full of clothes, my toothbrush, and deodorant, and a second bag with my fully-charged laptop next to the door. Ellie changed boots and picked out a ridiculous bright yellow knit hat with a massive white pompom flopping around on top.

She grinned. "I like it. It's sunny."

Sunny was what we needed, right now. I kissed her temple and I returned to the kitchen to get my axe.

Salvation did her version of a waking-up yawn when I lifted her off the top of the kitchen cabinets. I could reach her easily up there, but the kids could not, and Maura had to get the step-stool. Not that any of us thought Akeyla would do something stupid with the magical axe. Sal was pretty darned sharp, though, and without an adult elf around to add a guard spell on her blade, Maura thought the high-up resting place was a good idea.

Sal liked it, too. She had "a view." She did have a straight line through the doors to the deck and lake, not that she could see anything, but it made her happy.

Except for me leaving her with the elves last night. That did *not* make her happy.

"I had other business," I said.

My other business was not important.

She hadn't noticed Ellie when we came in, or anything out of the ordinary, though she was well aware of fae magic in the area. She was much more annoyed that I had not come home last night. Normally, I wouldn't care, but this edging toward a more possessive version of being "hers" was not sitting well with me.

"I have a girlfriend now," I said.

Sal had never met this mythical girlfriend and demanded an opportunity to magically vet the mystery woman. She wanted me to remember I needed to be careful. I had Akeyla to consider. Sophia and Jax, as well. The entire town. What if some harpy tried to mimic a real woman and used her entrancing wiles on me? Brother had been bad enough. My axe was not going to tolerate anyone else causing me damage.

I stood in the middle of my kitchen, Sal in one hand and my truck keys in the other, with my usually not-so-chatty magical artifact huffing and puffing about how mean I was for not considering her feelings when entering into a situation with a possibly menacing and dangerous other woman.

Ellie leaned against the wall into the hallway. She sniffed and shook her head. "I was hoping you breaking the concealments would extend to your axe." She waved her hand. "Since a lot of her sensing of the world is done through you."

I shrugged.

Sal thought I shrugged at her, and tossed me yet another jolt of huffiness.

"This is the first time I've ever been glad you can't actually talk," I said.

I got the distinct impression that she was working on the whole talking thing.

"What?" I asked.

Her talking was not important right now. My unwanted and unnecessary girlfriend was.

"Did you just push into my head that my girlfriend is unnecessary?"

Ellie chuckled. "At least your dog likes me."

Sal responded with more huffing.

"You've met her, Sal," I said. "She's here, right now."

Sal insisted she had not met any new female friend, romantic or otherwise, and that she and I were the only two standing in the kitchen.

"Do you remember the fae magic in Vampland?" I asked. "The fae magic that helped you get back to me?" Without Ellie and Sal, I would have died in a pocket land full of vampires.

She did.

"Well?" I asked.

If my axe had eyes, she would have narrowed them at me.

"Her name is—" And I couldn't get it out. *Helpful fae magic* somehow managed to circumvent the concealments, as did referring to Ellie as *her* and *my girlfriend*, but her name was still not allowed.

"Did she sense the dryads?" Ellie asked.

"Have you sensed any other fae magic?" I asked Sal. "There were two dryads sniffing around."

She had noticed fae magic outside just before I came in and she would like to make a report to King Odinsson. The fae were dangerous. Even helpful fae. I was to be careful. She did her version of a frown. *You're mine*, she tossed into my head.

"Yes, yes, my dear," I said. "But if this all works out, that helpful fae magic will introduce you to another helpful magical artifact." I held her out in front of me and twirled her a few times, an activity that caused both her and Akeyla the same amount of enjoyment. "Don't you want to make friends?"

Why would she want friends? All the other artifacts were stupid.

I chuckled. "She says she doesn't care to make friends because everyone else is stupid," I said to Ellie.

My girlfriend shook her head. "You have no idea how happy I am that my camera isn't showing signs of jealousy."

My axe was like some sort of maturing magical artificial intelligence. "You really have grown, haven't you?" I asked.

I walked toward Ellie and the front door. "The elves," I said to Sal, "seem busy."

A sense of *miffed* flowed off my axe. She sensed the so-called helpful fae magic again, and she would not talk of elven secrets when a fae might steal a golden and tender morsel of knowledge.

I stopped just into the hallway, probably more shocked by Sal's poetics than I was by those of the dryads.

Ellie walked to the front door and shouldered her backpack. "What?" she asked.

You may be enthralled manifested in my head. The words, the intent, the unease. "Sal..." I could hand her over to Akeyla, but I suspected if I did so, she would no longer consider me "hers." And even though she and I hadn't been in any battles with trolls or ogres, I felt better having her with me.

One day, I might need to face Brother again. "We aren't dealing with vampires," I said.

I handed Ellie the truck keys. She jostled her backpack and picked up the bag she'd filled with Maura's cast-off winter clothes. "I'll put these in Bloodyhood," she said.

She opened the front door and a puff of cold air blew into the entry.

Sal wanted to know why I'd left the door open.

"How are we going to deal with this?" I muttered. How to prove to my axe that Ellie wasn't the threat here? I had no idea what to do.

I hoisted my two bags and followed Ellie out. We tucked all the bags behind the passenger seat. "I'm going to put you in your pocket. Okay?" I asked Sal. She liked to ride in the cab. Usually. "Unless you want to be out in the cold."

Sal did her version of a sniff. I was clearly prioritizing the helpful fae magic.

"I'm not going to leave you behind."

The helpful fae magic was close again. It made her tingle, which she didn't like, but she carried no fear.

That bit of understanding extended to all things: Sal feared nothing and no one. She was my Salvation.

There had to be some way to rein in her possessiveness. At this point, I suspected simply giving her to Akeyla wouldn't work.

I tucked my jealous axe into her pocket. "We're going to the hospital," I said. "You'll be fine."

Ellie shook her head and waited next to the door.

Sal sniffed again.

Ellie hopped into the passenger side and closed the door as I walked around and got in to drive.

My phone rang.

"Where have you been, son?" Arne's angry voice boomed into my ear. I pulled the phone away and mouthed *Arne* as I got into the truck.

"I…" I grunted. Damned concealments. I put the phone on speaker.

"Never mind." Arne said it with such speed I suspected he knew why I couldn't say. "The wolves are sleeping off the run." After a Samhain full moon run, the wolves would likely sleep all day, not so much because they wanted to, but because that's what the magic demanded. Gerard and Remy would be awake and available by early evening. Axlam, too, though I hoped that after her injuries inside St. Martin's evil wolf magic, both her pack and the elves would make her rest another day.

"All's well, wolf-wise?" I asked, just to make sure.

"Other than Lennart pulling in Ed in the middle of the blizzard, yes." The annoyance in his voice was neither surprising nor all that harsh. Lennart would be on the receiving end of a lecture about mundane safety during wolf runs, and Arne would be on the receiving end of words from Ed about the safety of his daughter. All of which was likely necessary.

"Tell him Sophia's touched," Ellie said.

"Sophia's touched," I said. "I saw the magic." A lie, since Ellie hadn't yet shown me any photos of Sophia and I hadn't seen any unaccounted-for magic when the kids came to help Axlam.

"Later," Arne snapped. He loudly exhaled. "If Rose's notebook grants you more of those magic-showing photos, please share."

Ellie twisted her head as if to say *See, he knows.* "Tell him about those dryads."

Arne sniffed as if, maybe, some of what Ellie said made it across the phone connection.

"We had fae visitors," I said. "Dryads came to speak to the trees."

Arne inhaled. "Fae? Now?" He exhaled. "They smell blood in the water," he muttered. "Damned prissy sharks."

"That's not very nice." Ellie pointed at the phone. "Maniacal and manipulative fae is a stereotype." She frowned. "Not all of us are prissy."

From behind the seat, Sal sent out a wave of understanding that felt very much like an ironic *but we have a helpful fae magic friend* to me.

I pinched the bridge of my nose, happy that my girlfriend could not hear my jealous axe's derisive comment.

"Did you say they Lorax-ed you?" Arne asked. "Oak sharks, those dryads," he muttered again.

In the two-hundred-plus years of my life in Alfheim, I had never before heard an elf become so Americanized as to verbize a proper noun. "They came to ask the trees questions," I said.

I swear I could hear Arne rubbing his face. "How many?"

"Two," I said. "They were in full armor. They were sucking up information about the magical events last night."

"They're offended. Samhain is important to them." He sighed. "Halfway between the equinox and the solstice is important to *all* magicals," he said.

And we'd just suffered major Samhain-adjacent events: St.

Martin's wolf, even the entirety of the episode with Brother and the vampires were themselves part of something bigger.

Like tornadoes in a hurricane.

The phone clicked. Arne was pacing an acoustic floor, probably a tiled hallway at the hospital. "They were... opaque... weren't they?"

"Yes." Quite opaque. "Lots of slight-of-hand and turning of phrases."

Arne *hmphed* much like my axe. "Fae," he said. "Wonderful."

Ellie blinked. "I took pictures after they left, King Odinsson," she said as if to quell his annoyance.

Arne sighed. "Listen, Frank," he said. "That little shit St. Martin snapped several of my wife's ribs. She has internal injuries requiring observation and recuperation. Fae poking around won't help handle the aftermath."

Part of me wasn't surprised, while another part wished Dagrun had trusted me more. "It wasn't a genie, Arne," I said. "Or fae."

Ellie shook her head. "It was wolf magic, sir. Strong wolf magic. I was worried about the kids when it showed up at Frank's place."

I swear I heard Arne kick something. "We know it wasn't a real djinn. Dag will be home in two or three days. When she's healed enough, we'll discuss this at The Hall."

The elven healers were keeping her for multiple *days*? How bad were her injuries? "She hid her wounds from me, Arne. If I'd known—"

"If you'd known, she still would have made you take Axlam to safety, son. You and I both know that."

We did. I did. But I likely would have gone back for Dag. I glanced at Ellie. This time, she squeezed my thigh. "I'll meet you at the hospital," I said. We could check on Dag.

"No," Arne snapped. He sighed again. "Not if you're a fae magnet, son. Best let Dagrun rest."

She'd be pulling IVs from her arm and yelling "I'm fine!" at the nurses if she got wind of yet another threat wafting into Alfheim.

"If you wish," I said.

"I need to rouse Magnus from his jetlag anyway. Meet me at his farm and I'll have him help you with this fae issue."

"Magnus is back from New Zealand?" I asked.

Arne hung up without answering.

"Magnus flew in during the blizzard?" Ellie asked.

Not that a blizzard would hamper our elder Freyr elf.

Ellie ran her fingers over her camera. "I'll stay in the truck when we get to his farm," she said, "so as not to interfere with the elves." She tapped the cantaloupe-sized piece of wood on her lap. "We'll need to go home so I can develop the plates I exposed."

She looked up at me expectantly.

I'd assumed me staying was now the default. But thinking about it —actually considering where I was going to sleep tonight—felt... nice. We were in the middle of a developing crisis and here I was calmer than I had any right to be because my brand-new relationship made me euphoric.

Ellie smiled. She leaned over the gearshift. "Thank you for figuring out how to get through the enchantments," she said.

I had no doubts about us. I'd found something worth fighting for. I would fight for it, too. Apprehension, though, continued to knock at the back of my brain. Apprehension that those two fae had sniffed her out, no matter how well her mother cast her enchantments.

I grinned anyway. "Do I get a drawer in the bathroom?"

She poked my thigh this time. "You know the cottage already added space for you next to the sink."

It had. I smiled.

But something was going to happen. Something always did. We were likely about to roll down Alfheim's roads toward that happening the moment I pulled the truck out of the driveway.

I had no idea how to stop it, or see it coming, or whether there'd be damage. Maybe the price of being all-in with fae magic would end up being too high. Maybe it'd be another outsider, like St. Martin, or the wolf magic that had masqueraded as St. Martin's "genie." I'd already run into a powerful Wolf that didn't like me. Why not two? I wasn't lucky enough in love or life for such damages to pass me on by.

If Ellie had seen anything coming in her photos, she would have said. I started up the truck, wondering if I was just being paranoid.

"You make me happy," Ellie said in a low, husky voice. She wiggled again. "So very *happy*."

My girlfriend was wiggling suggestively in the passenger seat of my truck.

Something else new and nice, even if it did sidetrack my poor, awestruck brain. "Beautiful, you are one distracting woman," I said.

A pop of annoyance rolled from Sal, followed by a declaration that she was sure I'd been enthralled by the so-called helpful fae magic.

I groaned and pulled out onto the road.

"What?" Ellie asked.

"My jealous axe."

Ellie chuckled. "You and I are going to be the best of friends, Salvation!" She nodded toward Sal's handle. "Just wait. It's going to be you and me against the world. And who better to train me in hand-to-hand?"

Sif the Golden would be better for training Ellie in any martial arts. Or either of our mothers.

Family, I thought, and drove us toward town.

CHAPTER 9

S hortly after Ed and his family moved to Alfheim, when they were first getting used to winters with snow, he'd told me how surprised he'd been at the speed with which the Minnesota Department of Transportation cleared the roads. The kids had expected snow days every other Tuesday. He'd expected chains on tires and blizzard conditions solid from the Winter Solstice to the Spring Equinox.

He was about a century too late for that. Winter life in modern Minnesota was more about keeping your wiper blades in good condition and making sure your boots were waterproof. Plus every year, a day or two after Samhain, Arne went out to the Alfheim County MnDOT Maintenance and Operations Depot and charmed all the plows.

He clearly hadn't done so yet this year.

The road from my place to Magnus's stables was close to impassable. As the sun moved into late afternoon and the temperature began its slow slide into nighttime chill, what had been snow was now crusty slush on its way to becoming ice. Bloodyhood handled it well, but Ellie did not.

The road curved. Bloodyhood's back end continued on in the direction we had been going while its front end compensated by going a little too far in the opposite direction.

These things happen when driving on ice. Bloodyhood is big, heavy, and brand-new, so it was just a little fishtail. I easily drove through it. Nothing to worry about.

Ellie sat ramrod-straight in her seat and white-knuckle-gripped the door. A little yip escaped her lips.

I was beginning to suspect that this was the first time her cottage had moved her into extreme winter conditions. Not that Minnesota had more than a few storms' worth of extreme conditions every year. "I'll teach you how to control a slide like that," I said.

Bloodyhood bounced along over the crackling ice, which did nothing to settle nerves or stomachs. Ellie stared out the windows, still gripping the door, with the yellow hat pushed up on her forehead so that the pompom brushed the headrest every time we hit a particularly deep rut in the ice.

"Foot off the accelerator. Eyes straight ahead. Don't overcorrect," I said. "We'll practice in a parking lot. It'll be fun."

She tossed me a *you cannot be serious* look.

Sal wanted me to know that she was picking up distinct waves of incredulousness from the so-called helpful fae magic. It might affect my enthralling. I was to be careful.

My axe was tattling on my annoyed girlfriend in order to protect me. I was in the middle of the most bizarre love triangle on Earth.

"Is the whole winter going to be like this?" Ellie asked.

What did Arne say about the fae? Sharks smelling blood in the water. The same thing happened in Alfheim when tourists asked the local mundanes about the weather. Eyes brightened. Lips curled ever so slightly. *We got a live one!* reverberated through the entire population and all that Minnesota Nice became the perverse thrill of egging on the cold-based terror of non-locals.

After two hundred years, that thrill affects me as well, but I held back the reflexive need to say the local favorite of "Just wait until

January when it's too cold to snow." Or the other popular response of "Shoveling too fast will give you a heart attack, ya know."

"You'll get used to it," I said.

She blinked three times. Her hand released from the door panel. Then she broke out into a hearty laugh. "One of the locals in Alice Springs said exactly the same thing about the heat." She tapped the tip of her nose. "Same expression. Same tone of voice." She shrugged. "Different accent."

I laughed, too.

"They had firenadoes."

I shrugged. "Snownadoes here."

Her eyes widened. "Seriously?"

I shook my head. "They're mostly snow dust devils. Except that one in spring of 1816. That wasn't fun."

She slumped back into her seat and adjusted the yellow hat and its big white pompom. "Can we move someplace with nice weather? California, maybe?"

I almost said "Earthquakes." But then I realized she'd just said *we*.

Why was I stunned? Because I was stunned. After this morning, the last thing I should be was stunned.

Yet my screaming raccoon was back, and this time, he was laughing.

Red crept up Ellie's jaw to her cheeks.

I reached across and took her gloved hand in mine. She looked down at our fingers, then up at my face with the same openness and vulnerability I'd seen in the kitchen this morning.

She squeezed my fingers. "Both hands on the wheel, handsome."

I'd never get used to *handsome*. If I was honest, I actually found it kind of annoying, in the same way I'd find *sweet widdle cuddle-bunny* annoying.

She let go of my hand and pointed down the road. "That's an animal transport."

It didn't take us long to catch up. We were behind at least five identical trucks. They were all inching along as if there was an accident up ahead. I peered around the trucks as best I could and sure enough, up ahead, cop lights reflected off the side of the lead eighteen-wheeler.

All the transports carried sheep. Big ones, too. Their *baaing* overpowered the roar of the truck's heater, so they weren't all that happy, even if they were fat, healthy, and giving off lots of indistinct flutters of magic that floated away through the slats.

"Who transports sheep in the winter?" Ellie asked. "And so many?"

The magic wafting from the transports wasn't unusual. We had a lot of magic-protected animals in Alfheim. "Elves," I said. Though moving sheep right after a blizzard seemed a bit reckless, even for elves.

The indistinct magic coming off the second truck flared just enough as we passed to make me squint.

Not everything the elves did was my business, but sometimes I wished the non-elder elves would tighten up their spellwork.

We inched forward to find Ed Martinez's cruiser in the middle of the road, lights on, blocking access to Magnus Freyrsson's grand stable and horse breeding operation. Red and blue flashed with a headache-inducing rhythmic cadence that bounced disjointedly off the snow.

All the trucks were turning onto Magnus's property. I really didn't think much of it, since Magnus did own the biggest and most prosperous farm in Alfheim County.

I stopped next to Ed's car and rolled down the window. "Arne sent me out." I pointed at the lovely hand-carved Freyrsson Stables sign and leaned a little out the window. "We might have a fae problem."

Ed frowned for a split second before his face returned to cop flatness. He'd switched out his normal brimmed Sheriff's hat for a beanie, and a large "Alfheim County Sheriff's Department" logo sat right between his eyes as if his detective sense had turned into a literal third eye.

He looked exhausted, too, with dark circles under his brown eyes, as if he hadn't slept. Which he probably hadn't, since he'd been pulled into the run. But at least he and his daughter were safe.

He glanced around me at Ellie. "Ma'am," he said.

"Ellie Jones," she said. "We've met but you don't remember me."

"Sophia does." The audible low noise that rolled from his body sounded as much like a growl as it did a groan. He looked up at the road as another transport rolled by from the other direction. "Stay away from my kids," he said.

This was not good. Not while we were dealing with yet another magical crisis. "Ed," I said.

He held up his hand. "My wife wants to move down to The Cities. Said at this point, I could come in as a Chief Deputy Sheriff in one of the suburban departments. I told her I'd talk to my contacts in Ramsey and Carver Counties."

Ellie leaned toward the window. "Sheriff Martinez, I'm—"

He waved her off. "I won't remember anything you say." He slapped Bloodyhood's door. "We have sixteen accidents this morning with the snow, and I'm here keeping tabs on freakin' *sheep* because Magnus Freyrsson thinks he's just as much in charge as Arne Odinsson. Go."

He'd dealt with vampires for us. He'd handled the mundane issues caused by Dracula and St. Martin. But none of that had affected his children. Putting himself in danger was one thing. His family? Absolutely not.

I nodded. "Let's talk later." I was the closest thing to another understanding mundane Ed had here in Alfheim.

He grunted and waved us through.

"How long has that been brewing?" Ellie asked. "And now he has a touched daughter."

"I don't know." Though he'd been frustrated with the elves for quite a while. Frustrated with the magic and the threats that came with it.

I should have been paying better attention. Ed was a friend.

I pulled Bloodyhood onto the wide plowed-and-salted drive to Magnus's village—because if I was honest, that's what it was.

Freyrsson Stables was its own localized economic engine, complete with multiple housing options—ranging from a set of understated townhomes for the stable staff and their families, to Magnus's old 1886 mansion which he'd turned into a bed and breakfast, to his massive new mansion hidden away in the trees from the farm's major dealings.

There were also meeting spaces hidden in the barns and buildings, because he liked to do a lot of his other business dealings here among his grand Percherons and Fjord horses. Nothing said "prosperous" to an investor like Magnus's gorgeous stallion, Bloodyhoof himself.

"Wow," Ellie said.

"This is why enclaves hoard their Freyr elves."

She pointed at the little café next to the tourist entrance to the horse barns. "There have to be rules about showing off like this."

"There are rules about personal enrichment. No greed. All wealth-building must be done in the service of the local economy." At least that's what Arne said. All the elves lived comfortably, but none of them skated through life on trust funds. Benta worked to benefit her sanctuary. Arne and Dag worked to build a prosperous Alfheim for the local mundanes. Even though we weren't one of the rich Metro suburbs, our schools were some of the best in the state.

And Magnus... well, Magnus Freyrsson worked all the time. Between the Stables, Gullinbursti Reclamations, the cargo plane business, the auto dealerships, and all his resorts and tourist businesses, Magnus was responsible for a significant portion of Alfheim's economic stability. So he wasn't showing off. He was signaling that this place was as much his Hall as it was our Odin elves'.

Arne's brand-new, blood-red, standard-issue electric Honda sat in front of one of the barns. Getting here before we did must have involved plenty of magic, especially with the roads, but there he was, leaning against the also-deep-red wall next to the door as if we were two hours late.

Right next to his Honda sat Magnus's also-brand-new, also-electric, midnight-blue Porsche Taycan.

Ellie pointed again. "Now, see, Oberon would string up his Second before he allowed him to drive a nicer car."

"I doubt Oberon's Second is a Freyr aspect," I said. Freyr aspects had exceptional taste in all things prosperous. "Having a Magnus as their Second is our King and Queen's way of showing off." Magnus Freyrsson could walk into any enclave on Earth and be its King within hours, yet he preferred to live here in small-town Minnesota with his buddies.

I parked off to the side out of habit. I handed Ellie my keys. "Just in case," I said.

She tucked them into her pocket.

Ellie laid her hand on her camera. "Should I take photos?"

She was worried about offending the elves. "The magic around this place is quite beautiful," I said. "The sheets of energy here are more like true aurora than most other magicks."

She grinned as if a warm memory had surfaced. "There's a place, in England somewhere, I don't remember where..." She did a small frustrated shake as if, like so many other memories manipulated by her enchantments, she couldn't quite recall what she wanted. "Anyway, it's a gateway into my mother's realm." She looked back at me. "The fae tend to make the ways into their realms enticing. Small, too, so only one person can pass through at a time, and to make them hard to find. But they're always eerie. And lovely." She waved her fingers. "Tingly and rush-inducing, like a rollercoaster."

I squeezed her fingers. "Sounds like the gate into The Great Hall."

Magnus Freyrsson stepped through the barn's door and out into the snow. If he had jetlag, he wasn't showing it in his glamour. He appeared impeccable, as one would expect of Magnus Freyrsson, except for the tastefully styled, zippered wool sweater jacket. It fit him perfectly and set off the silver rings and the chain around his neck, yet screamed in a bold black, white, and red stylized wave-turbulence pattern shot through with tiny lines of blue, green, and yellow.

He rolled his shoulders and frowned as if he noticed Bloodyhood, but didn't notice because Ellie watched him from the cab, and the whole confusion made him sad.

Ellie sucked in her breath. "I forgot how handsome he is," she muttered. "Even in his glamour."

Every one of my facial muscles tightened. I squinted and the part of my upper lip directly below my nose tried to yank my mouth into an angry sneer all because Ellie commented on a phenomenon as natural and true as the sunset.

Magnus Freyrsson was exceptionally beautiful, even for an elf. He'd been a silent movie star. Mundanes loved him. He brought joy and success to Alfheim. And he'd given me my wonderful new truck.

But still.

Ellie's eyes widened. "You're jealous! Oh, Frank." She leaned across the gearshift and kissed my cheek. "He's *terrifying*. They both are."

I blinked. "What?" Magnus wasn't scary, and Arne was less terrifying than Dag.

She kissed me again, then pointed. "They're staring at the truck wondering where you are."

Arne and Magnus couldn't see me in the cab because of Ellie's enchantments. She stroked my arm. "Don't take too long."

"I won't." I didn't want to get out of the truck no matter how much I needed to talk to the elves. Honestly, I just wanted to go back to the cottage and stow my toiletries in my brand-new bathroom drawer.

Perhaps fatigue was finally hitting, except I didn't fatigue. Not physically. My semi-dead body liked its baseline homeostasis and it took a lot of effort to move my needle. Hence all the whiskey when I was with Benta. And my viability as a battery to power Dracula's vampire swarm spells.

Mentally, though, Samhain and its run-up had me wishing for wine, a good book, and an evening of Ellie cuddles.

"Salvation," I said, "time to talk to our King."

My axe wanted to know if the helpful-yet-untrustworthy fae magic was going to stay in the truck.

"Yes, Sal." How could an axe be so annoying?

Well then, they should go talk to the elves, and I was the annoying one, not her.

"Are you two arguing?" Ellie pulled out her camera and exposed a plate as I pulled Sal from her pocket. "I bet the magic flowing between you two has its own unique intricacy."

Sal wanted to know if there was another artifact in the truck. Another artifact was proof I was enthralled.

I rolled my eyes. "Let's go talk to the elves," I said, and with my axe in hand, I stepped out of Bloodyhood to learn just how badly off post-Samhain Alfheim really was.

CHAPTER 10

Arne was pinching his brow as I walked up. Magnus, though, grinned like the party-loving Freyr elf that he was, and threw his arms wide. "Mr. Victorsson! Where were you hiding, young man?"

Up close, parts of the design on Magnus's jacket looked suspiciously like pointy elf ears, and others looked as if someone had pulled in hints of Yggdrasil.

He smoothed his hands over his chest. "I got this beauty from an ocean spirit on the North Island." Then he smoothed each arm. "It's a new pattern, one the local magicals created to signify their dealings with us elves." He nodded once. "Best New Zealand wool money can buy. I brought home several, Mr. Victorsson, if you'd like one."

Arne groaned.

Magnus shot him a look. "You know damned well they come with a sizing spell."

"I take it your trip was a success?" I switched Sal to my other shoulder.

Magnus laughed and slapped my upper arm. "Most definitely!" He leaned closer and winked. "Strengthened our ties to our Icelandic brothers and sisters, as well."

He must have literally charmed the pants off of Þórdís Ullrsdottir, the Icelandic elf who accompanied him to New Zealand in order to keep his more adoration-cult-starting behaviors under control.

"We have other business, Magnus," Arne said. He slapped the side of the barn as if to remind us that we were still standing out in the cold.

Magnus pouted like a little kid. "But I brought Bjorn goats." He pointed at the livestock transports as they passed by the tourist barns on their way toward the actual pastures father down the service road.

I realized why the magic wafting off all those sheep transports had been so bright and bold, like Magnus's sweater.

"You brought the sheep from New Zealand?" I couldn't disguise the incredulousness in my voice any more than I could keep it from showing on my face. "How many?"

He shrugged. "A thousand? I lost count when they added the bees."

"*Bees?*" He brought home bees?

Magnus sighed, very much the way Akeyla did when she thought I was being obtuse. "We'll ship the insects in later. It's winter here."

"How the hell did you get a thousand sheep through customs?" I blurted out.

"Enough!" Arne slapped the wall again. "No more talk of your sheep, Magnus Freyrsson! I told you we have problems. Fae showed up."

Magnus's demeanor abruptly shifted. His innate sheets of magic brightened and thickened as if they'd solidify around his body like ice.

How long had Arne been here before we drove up? I'd obviously stepped into the middle of an ongoing argument.

Magnus went from joyously talking up his trade exploits to a laser-focused warrior. "Oh, we have all *sorts* of *fae* problems, don't we, Arne Odinsson?"

Ellie was right. He was terrifying.

Arne's magic also brightened, and for a split second, I was sure he was about to whip a bolt of lightning at Magnus's head. "Are *you* going to clean up all the sheep dung?"

"I'm the one with the barns and stables, now aren't I?"

"What are you two doing?" I was caught between the All-Father and Uncle Freyr while they argued about the elven equivalent of snowblower sparkplugs and the coming season more than any of the real horrors pressing against Alfheim.

And like a lot of such arguments, it wasn't about any snowblower. Or sheep. Or stables and barns. It was about whose driveway needed clearing most, and first, and the family, and who was in charge.

Magnus called up a ball of magic. It floated just above his hand, so thick it probably threw a shadow strong enough for a mundane to notice. It looked like a milky glass orb to me, one full of something so powerful the ball needed to hide it, even from my ability to see magic.

Every single elder elf in Alfheim had the power and magic to run the enclave. Bjorn especially and Magnus particularly. Benta too, and the handful of other old elves; all had elevated magic and knowledge that could all bring the world to its knees.

I knew this intellectually. They were the elves who had built the realm around The Great Hall. They protected the town. But only three times had I seen them armored-up and in battle. Never had I seen them fight amongst themselves.

The throwdown in Las Vegas didn't count. Even there, they restrained their power. But something let loose here.

"Like Alfheim needs protection, King?" Magnus drawled.

The loose something, the unlacing of the constraints the elves use in order to operate among mundanes, revealed a truth none of them had ever before allowed me to see.

I'd long wondered if, when an elf was out of glamour, they were actually making their full nature visible. If out-of-glamour meant elf-in-Midgard and not elf-as-true-elf, and if this was the real reason some of them had a difficult time with glamouring. If powering what was essentially two glamours took more fine-grained control than many of them could manage.

If they were all, on some level, walking around inside their own personal concealment enchantments.

Magnus's words, his drawl, hit Arne like Thor's hammer. Something cracked.

I suspected Arne hadn't slept in the last thirty-six hours. He hadn't rested after the run and he'd just come from the hospital after his wife —his Queen and his mate—suffered injuries so severe she was not going to be released for at least a few days. We had unknown fae lurking around. And his town and enclave were threatened not only by St. Martin's "genie," but also by some other threat he had not yet shared with me.

The All-Father appeared. Only for a blink of the eye, but long enough to cause me to squint and for Sal to let out a small yip.

The elf standing next to the door leading into his Second's domain was still Arne Odinsson. Still the khaki-wearing semi-retired husband of Alfheim's mayor. Still the big but balding glamour he wore when out and about. He was also King Odinsson, the elf with the notched ear and the lynx for a pet. He was all versions of the man who called me "son."

But he was also Magic. He was the personification of the sacrifice that had driven his god to hang from Yggdrasil in search of wisdom. He gave and he protected and he stood between the worst of the world and his children.

And then, like the flash from the folding magic, it was gone.

"Magnus…" he said.

The other elf stood perfectly still and spoke quietly but with great force. "You *promised*, Odinsson. You told us when we left our enclaves that this new land would bring us a new way. That we had nothing to fear."

Arne walked toward Magnus. "I still hold that promise, my brother." He glanced at me as he moved by and gave my shoulder a quick squeeze.

Ellie stared through the windshield as if the moment's display had frightened her so much she wanted to hide.

Arne gripped Magnus's shoulders. "You don't know what happened during the run." He glanced back at me. "What was revealed to Dagrun."

He meant Ellie's photos. The ones that showed conclusively that St. Martin's magic was wolf magic.

Magnus did not move. "I drove into Alfheim at the height of the moon last night. I smelled *all* the magicks on the blizzard winds," he said. "You said the concealment enchantments would do their job."

Magnus knew about Ellie's concealments? I opened my mouth but once again, nothing came out.

Not from me.

Sal burst out with how she thought I was enthralled by a so-called helpful fae magic that had also helped her in Vampland. We all needed to be careful.

The two elves turned toward me. "What did you say, Salvation?" Arne said.

The helpful fae magic was in my truck. She had an artifact. I kept telling Salvation that I was in a relationship with the magic but she was not convinced.

"Is this true, Frank?" Arne asked.

"I…" Nothing would come out.

Sal had noticed my inability to speak the name of the tentatively helpful magic in the presence of elves. Which meant I had to be enthralled.

Magnus stared at Arne again. "The enchantments are in place to protect us." He said his words slowly and with more than a little threat in them.

Ellie said she thought they knew about her.

No no no, I thought. The elves had always been good about taking in strays. They took me in. But maybe a fae-born seer was too much fae. Or too much witch. And if they learned who her mother was…

I stepped back from the two elves.

They were talking about promises and dangers they'd never deemed worthy of sharing with me. Dangers they considered concealed. A danger behind concealment enchantments.

Was this what Ed felt? Powerless in the face of forces over which he had no control? As sheriff, if anyone was supposed to have a handle on how to figure out and navigate forces, it was Ed. Until they came for his family.

All this damned well better not come for Ellie.

I had no idea at all if she was in harm's way. No idea if Ed's kids were truly in harm's way, either. But the chance was there, and more real than the agitation and anxiety the chaos of this moment generated in my buzzing senses.

Calm was not the way of magic. You could carve out calm moments, but soon enough nature would rail against you again in tooth and claw, blood and bone. The chance it had just come for Ellie was too much.

I dropped Sal onto the cleared walk in front of the barn door. She clanked against the concrete, bounced twice, and landed on her side at Arne's feet.

Surprise ricocheted from her to Arne, and back, as if she'd figured out what she'd just done.

"That fae magic *helped* you, Salvation," I said.

Friend… Sal pushed out as if she was running the numbers and picking pluses and minuses.

Magnus blinked. His lips rounded, then he let out a loud burst of laughter. "Friend? Oh, you sweet axe, you."

Arne shot him a look that said pure *Silence!*

Here I was in the middle of a magical storm centered around complicated magic the elves believed was not my business.

My girlfriend was my business.

I looked back at the truck and Ellie waiting in the passenger seat. All the seismic shifting that was happening here wasn't just the argument between Arne and Magnus. It was also my priorities.

The Elf King of Alfheim leaned closer to Magnus. "We will speak inside."

"I'm leaving," I said.

Surprise danced across Arne's face. It jumped to Magnus, who blinked.

There was no leaving this behind, no matter how my priorities might change. But until then, I saw no real reason to put myself or Ellie in the path of the magic.

But... rolled from Sal.

I ignored her and turned toward the truck.

The wind picked up and a resurgence of winter cold slapped me across the face. Or perhaps it was a different cold I felt. Either way, I'd had enough of it for the morning.

CHAPTER 11

E llie stared through Bloodyhood's windshield, wide-eyed and clutching her camera to her belly, as if she thought Arne and Magnus were going to nuke each other and spread a magical Armageddon across the entire of the state of Minnesota.

"I got a picture of King Odinsson." She looked at me, eyes still wide, and paler than she should be. "After Magnus… changed." She looked back at me. "I've seen glamours shift like that before. In Tokyo with the kami. Fae, too. Spirits when I was in Australia. It's like subtle body language. I think they can't always keep their emotions from manifesting in their magic." She inhaled. "Even elder elves like the King and his Second. I figured something might show on a photo. Something in the future that I can see. So I took a picture."

She couldn't see Arne's Odin aspect the way I did, but she clearly felt it. "He went All-Father," I said.

"Yeah." She fiddled with the camera and carefully tucked it into the backpack. "Yeah, he did." She looked up. "You left Sal with the elves?"

I started the truck. "Yes." I'd explain about Sal later. Ellie needed to know what Magnus said. "You were right. They know about you." I put Bloodyhood into drive and rolled toward the road. "Or at least about your concealment enchantments."

"Yeah." She ran her fingers over her camera without saying what we both knew was true: At least one Royal Fae Court had taken notice of Alfheim, and it was likely our fault. My fault, for being elf-adjacent and breaking through her concealment enchantments.

This was worse than Brother and the vampires. Worse than that sniveling little Renfield of a worm St. Martin coming around to hurt Axlam and the town. This was as chaotic and terrifying as the night I woke on my father's lab table: I had no clue what was happening, or why forces had descended to cause so much pain, or what to do to make it to stop.

My father had not wanted me. He'd abandoned me to the storms, and I'd panicked.

Not this time. I was no longer alone. Like Sal said, I had family to consider and a girlfriend the elves clearly did not see as a bonus to Alfheim.

"I..." I inhaled. How to tell her about my fears without sounding overbearing? "I don't think the elves are happy."

Ellie frowned.

"Magnus is itching for a fight." Was I? No. I'd had enough violence to last me my two-and-a-half mundane lifetimes. "Arne seemed more..." I wasn't quite sure. Resigned, perhaps. Tired, for sure.

"Weary of the battle to come," Ellie said.

A battle that made Ellie a target.

I'm not some kid who's fallen in love for the first time, I thought. I needed to stay calm but *threat* was wedging between my lungs and my ribcage. Keeping my muscles from tensing was taking considerable effort. And those damned lights were dancing around in the cabin now.

Because it wasn't a sense of threat I felt. Or even a panic I could name and thus control like the demon it was. No, this was a holistic *threat* as if the buzzing and squirming of my internal organs was itself a thing. A presence. A real, deeper-than-my-body, all the way to my soul connection.

As if I felt all threats to Ellie in my bones because...

The lights in my peripheral vision weren't just my overwhelmed brain. They were magic.

I didn't look at her. I made sure she couldn't see my lack-of-poker-face.

The threat triggered something that was probably in the process of triggering anyway. Because I was all-in. Because…

Because the elves' animosity to her concealment enchantments was a threat to my mate.

Why was this happening? I wasn't a werewolf. We hadn't been together twenty-four hours yet. We were in the phase of newness where my corpse-cold mornings were still a novelty and Ellie hadn't yet formed an informed opinion about just how much she could tolerate. What she'd accept. From me. From the elves and the town and her own family. From the cottage. From the entire magical world. And here I was dusting her with mate magic because I feel way too easily.

And now elven—and fae—disapproval threatened *my mate*.

My mate. I drove toward Alfheim with eyes on the icy road but the magic sparking around my hands was *obvious*.

"You okay?" Ellie asked.

I felt both the *hell-yes* okay and *hell-no* intolerable swirling in an ever-tightening whirlwind in my gut.

She dug in the pack again. "I'm going to take a picture of you." She pulled out her camera. "To make sure nothing happened while you were with the elves."

"No," I said. *Don't frighten Ellie*, I thought.

She stopped with her hand over the zipper. "Why?"

I needed an excuse. "How many plates did you bring?"

She sat back. "I have two more in my portfolio and six more at home." She stared at my hands. "The cottage will make more tonight."

"What if it doesn't?" Fill out that excuse. "Maybe I drained its reserves with the sunroom."

Her lips pulled into a tight line. "I can make more myself. I have a box of blanks in the library and the chemicals I need in the darkroom."

Excuses, excuses. "How long does it take you to make and polish a plate?"

She sighed and looked away. "Fine," she said.

She'd figure it out sooner or later. Hopefully after a nice calm meal and a nice calm evening discussing deep life-melding issues like whose mugs go in which cabinet.

I'm too old for this, I thought. Too old to be this frazzled and too old to be this overwhelmed. I'd been in relationships before. None of this was new to me.

Except the mate magic. I thought only the wolves had this fated-mate insta-romance chaos.

I did not like chaos. Chaos reminded me too much of my pre-Alfheim life. Of the abuses of my father, and the near-universal horrified reactions to my presence exhibited by every single mundane I came across. The dramatic screaming. The running away. The inability to consider and ask questions. To not judge.

Sort of like the elves and Ellie's concealments.

"Frank," she said. "I don't think you're okay."

My knuckles had turned bright white. The steering wheel creaked.

I let go. We drove along the road with my jittery hands hovering over the wheel. "I'm sorry," I said.

She slowly exhaled. "I know why you say that," she said.

I grasped the wheel and turned toward the lake. "What?"

"Say that you're sorry. You say it because you're huge and strong and expecting everyone who sees you to run away like terrified toddlers."

She was correct.

"You expect *me* to run away the first moment you accidently slip your self-imposed rules for how a mundane man is supposed to be."

She was correct about that, too. I knew how I needed to act.

"Not your rules about how a man should act—those are great, by the way. You're what I hope Jax grows up to be."

"Jax's upbringing isn't up to me," I said.

"Yes, it is. You're a part of his life. So are Arne Odinsson and

Magnus Freyrsson. Lennart Thorsson too, now that he's Jax's mate's soon-to-be stepdad."

This time I did glance at her.

"Seer, remember? Some things are so obvious I don't need my stone to spell them out for me."

And what did that mean for us? Me? I didn't ask. I kept my mouth shut. No need to be desperate.

"Your rules for action aren't the problem, Frank. It's your rules for being."

I had one set of rules. "Action and being are the same thing," I said.

Ellie returned to staring at the road. "Not when you're being for the sake of others."

"Still the same thing," I said as I turned off onto the small service road that led into the lake's peninsula. This way, I could park close to the cottage and out of sight of my cabin, so as not to confuse Maura into thinking I was home.

"The month you spent trying to break my concealments? I spent that time wishing for an excuse *not* to miss you. To be over you and to be okay and maybe somehow force the cottage to take me somewhere I wouldn't see you every day. Because I did, Frank. I saw you with the kids and the wolves and the elves. I took pictures of you hoping I'd find something in the layers of your life that told me to stay away." She shrugged. "Mostly that's why I took pictures."

She'd been nearby the entire time I was looking for a way through. But I knew that. We'd crossed paths several times. Each time I'd apologize for not remembering and promise to do better. Then she'd cry.

I parked in a small clearing closer to her cottage than to my cabin. "Mostly?"

"I like taking pictures of you." She tipped her head to the side. "You're big and handsome and *exactly* what I want."

I wasn't. How could I be? I was the stitched-together son of a mad scientist. I was forged from the parts of others. "Me" wasn't a singularity the way it was for a man born. And I certainly was not handsome.

She shook her head as she pulled the door handle. "I love you,

Frank Victorsson," she said. Then she was gone, out the door, walking toward a cottage I didn't know—nor could I explain—any better than my own self.

The dichotomy of *threat* returned to my gut. *My mate loves me* swirled with *My mate walked away.*

And once again, I had no idea what to do.

CHAPTER 12

"Ellie!" I followed her through the trees toward the cottage. The white pompom on her yellow hat bounced along like a snowball in the air, out ahead, about ten paces up the trail.

"Ellie!" I called again.

She stopped next to a huge, crooked cedar. The tree leaned a little more toward the lake with each storm but it continued to stand. It had its ways, the tree, and it did just fine.

We were under an umbrella of melting snow and the occasional drip hit the ice with more of a *splot* than anything twinkling or angelic. At least the mate magic had calmed down and wasn't sparking around my hands anymore.

"Ellie," Two paces away, maybe three, and I reached out.

She vanished. Gone. No signs. No footprints. Nothing, as if the cottage had called her back. Except we were a good five to six hours from sunset.

"Ellie!" I roared. The cottage was just up ahead, closer to the lake and behind the thicker stand. If the cottage closed, I still had a moment. I could still—

My mate magic flared up around me like one of the firenadoes Ellie had seen in Australia. I stopped and thrust out my hands as if to hold off ghosts as the flare coiled around me, then outward in little arms to the spot where Ellie should have been.

She hadn't vanished. I felt her—the mate magic felt her—but she was just out of reach as if she'd rounded a corner. I knew she was nearby but I couldn't see to touch.

My screaming racoon? He was back. But this time, he was screaming because he'd already ridden the raft over the falls and his calm river downstream had become a black hole.

I was lost again. Lost in my own shock and fear, and my own navigation of the chaos. Lost in need and desire because even though I thought I'd trained myself to *not* let my emotions flow easily—that I'd added enough locks and dams to even out those rushing rapids—I wasn't nearly as good at that part of living as I wanted to believe.

The need to hit a tree roared up my spine into my arm. A bellow rose in my throat.

The mate magic dust filled the cracks in my control and were about to blast past my façade of civility.

Because that's what it was. A façade. Yes, I had my ways of living, my code, but deep inside I was still that screaming child in a monster's body who awoke in my father's lab. Still that trauma. Still that pain.

Circumstances can be transcended, but they do not go away.

What was worse? The fact that I understood I was breaking apart, or the actual breaking? The watching myself implode, or the imploding? All because the mate magic swirling around my body carried a need as strong as breathing that I could not satisfy.

My air. My life. My angel. All things that I could not, should not, would *not* saddle Ellie with. Yet here I was with those wishes coiling around me like a whirlwind made of my own psyche.

I understood, yet I was utterly confused.

Why did I think this would be easy? Hope that after playing the odds with the universe, my good numbers had finally come up? I was a fool. But I'd already established that. I was a fool in love.

By all the pantheons of all the magicals everywhere on Earth, that mate magic tornado hurt. It burned like my morning cold, and like that cold, only Ellie's touch brought relief.

You know, the exact opposite of a trickster god's irritation.

My back stiffened. My senses heightened. And I immediately held out my arms in a defensive posture.

Nothing had changed about the woods. The snow continued to crackle and snap as it melted under the late afternoon sun. Birds chirped. Squirrels scurried and a small band of whitetail deer watched me from a respectable distance into the trees.

Yet for some reason the thought of tricksters overrode my Ellie implosion.

And yet there was nothing here out of the ordinary. The lake sloshed just beyond the trees. A few cars rumbled by on the road behind me. The animals acted in their animal ways. None of them seemed startled.

No response from Ellie, whom I was sure was still just out of reach. I yelled her name again.

Somewhere, in the trees between my truck and the cottage, someone giggled.

"Ellie!" I ran toward the cottage. Maybe if I got inside the gate, her concealments would cancel whatever spell hid her from me.

Cold wind slapped at my face and melting snow sloshed under my boots. Twigs snapped. A crow screeched as if it, too, had been startled by a trick neither of us understood. Magic wisps coiled around the trees and pushed through the brambles until I...

... crossed a threshold. Punctured a bubble. Ran through a barrier or veil or some other magical layer so thin I didn't see it until I was literally inside it.

Elven magic announced itself. It shimmered like the auroras and it danced around them and their works as if fully willing to take responsibility for what it did. But this... this was just like the membrane I crossed the first night I entered Ellie's cottage. This snuck in red and green, and tooth and claw. It was alive and *living*.

Hiding Ellie. Goading me to run.

A fae had set out a trap.

I inhaled, trying to right myself against this new, bountiful veil magic that felt more joyous than the malevolent carapace that had been manipulating St. Martin.

An elf manifested directly in front of me. His black eyes widened and his gray ponytail swayed. He gasped and touched his hand to his lips. "It worked!"

We'd met before, this elf and I. He was the one who'd helped me find Ellie's cottage. The one who'd said he was Arne's son. I'd mostly forgotten about him until now.

He extended his hand. "Hrokr Arnesson," he said. "I knew that once you broke my semi-sister's enchantments that I could rig a spell to extend that breaking to me."

This elf stood between me and my mate.

I could backfill the holes in my life—my *soul*—with elven family connections. With helping raise my niece. With my calm and accepted life in Alfheim. But there was a price. An exchange, an offering of *me* so that I could stay a part of *them*.

It's a good deal, as such deals go. I have community here. Family. But the mate magic swirled up into a vortex as if it was the living, breathing, about-to-break heart in my chest. It scoured my face. It raked my skin. It sandblasted my bones and all I felt was the bitter micro-bites of a life without Ellie.

I'd spent all of my pre-Alfheim days in that pit wailing and clawing and flailing as if I knew how to climb my way back into the sunshine. And now this elf had dropped a barrier between me and *us*.

Hrokr frowned and withdrew his hand, carefully wiping his palm on the black leather of his pants as if he'd just realized he'd offered me a filthy palm. He stared at his hand for a moment as if he really did believe he'd offered me a sticky, gooey handshake.

"Listen, Mr. Victorsson, my friend, I—"

He wasn't looking at me, nor did I think he was aware of my feral cyclone of mate magic.

I had my hand around his neck before he could choke out the rest of his sentence. "Reverse the spell you used to hide Ellie."

He blinked and opened his mouth as if I was actually choking him, and spread his hands wide to show compliance. "Sure, sure," he said. "No problem."

I loosened my grip.

"Well ... there's a *slight* problem." He held up his hand with tiny gap between his thumb and forefinger. "The spell lines up her enchantments with mine in such a way that someone who's broken *one* of the concealments—that would be you, big guy—can see *one* of us. It's a wave crest-and-trough thing. So see me or see her, and we have business." He shrugged.

I picked him up by his neck. He dangled off my arm, his hands gripping my wrist so he wouldn't choke, and gargled out his words.

"You're technically inside my concealments!" he gurgled. "Hurt me and you'll stay the jotunn of Alfheim no one can bother to remember!"

He was lying. He *had* to be lying. "A Loki elf lies. How original." I gave him a good shake.

"It was the only way!" he snorted out. "You're the only one in Alfheim who cares enough about us hiddens and undesirables to help! Plus you're the only one who broke one of the enchantments, so it's not like I had a choice."

I snatched his arm and whipped him around, arm pulled up and against the black leather of his hunting tunic, and pushed him face-first into the nearest tree trunk. "If she's hurt, I *will* snap your neck," I growled.

Violence is no longer my way, but my bulk and strength add credence to any threats, which are often more valuable than any actual violence.

"You will *not*." He rolled his eyes. "What would Ellie say? All your big and scary-handsome won't save you from *that* particular bit of bad behavior, now will it?"

I let go of his arm and allowed him to turn around, but I kept a grip on his wrist to keep him from casting spells. "I see magic, Loki elf. You try anything and I'll smash every bone in your hand." Even if he didn't believe me, the threat still stood.

"Yes, yes, Victorsson smash. I get it." He turned around to face me. "Will you listen now? Please? We don't have a lot of time."

I needed to keep my attention on the elf, but my body and soul cried out for Ellie. "What do you want?"

There had to be a way to tamp down the mate magic, otherwise Gerard and Remy would be utterly insufferable every moment Axlam and Portia Elizabeth were out of sight. Which they kind of were, to be honest. The extra wound-up tension was distracting.

I was not a werewolf. I could keep a grip on my emotions.

Hrokr rubbed his wrist when I let go. "There are fae around. They don't like me, and my dear father seems to be too busy to give a damn."

"Why do you want my help?" The last thing I needed was to knowingly piss off the fae *and* the elves by helping a Loki elf, especially one who lived behind concealments. Because the elves put this Loki elf where he couldn't bother anyone for a reason.

Hrokr stared out into the trees. "Those two dryads? The ones who were sniffing around your cabin? They were looking for me."

No, they weren't, I thought. My gut said *no,* but I had zero evidence pointing toward another reason.

My gut also told me that Alfheim was about to get sprayed with the shrapnel created by several fae-involved bombshells.

"Why?" I asked.

He looked in the opposite direction, as if he thought the two dryads would manifest at any second. He inhaled. "I'm half fae." He said it as if I was supposed to understand why I should care.

Tornadoes in a hurricane, I thought. "And I'm supposed to help you how?" I said. I might be almost seven feet tall, strong, and scary like he said, but if Oberon came calling, I'd be David to his Goliath. And Alfheim harbored not one half-fae slight to his Fae King honor, but two.

Hrokr here had just made *his* slight one of my problems.

He pouted.

"What do you *want?*" I asked again.

He ducked down and peered through a bush as if the two dryads were about to manifest out of the cold waters of my lake. "Isn't it obvious?"

"No," I said.

He sniffed the air. "Could you ask Miss Ellie Jones if I could, perhaps, *possibly* spend a night or two in her library until Oberon's goons go away?"

He wanted to hide in Ellie's library? The one room the cottage had not even deemed me worthy of seeing? The room that wasn't there but was?

"Absolutely not," I said.

Even on a good day, the last thing the world needed was a Loki elf —and Hrokr here was clearly one hundred percent a Loki elf— hanging out in a magical fae library that charged up overnight.

His lip quivered. He was Arne's size and build, with the same basic shape to his face, and the quivering lip was just too much. I snorted.

He grinned. "See?" He pointed at me again. "You like me! We're friends! I helped you out. I helped the kids. All I'm asking is just a few days somewhere out of Grandpa's reach."

"Tit for tat, huh?" I said.

All the friendliness drained from his posture. His face hardened. "I might trick, but I don't kill." He huffed and slapped his chest with his hand. "Yes, I'm an aspect of Loki but I'm not Tov Lokisson! I'm not malicious for maliciousness's sake. I'm me. I'm the protector of the vulnerable. That's what my mother wanted of me. She asked me to be *me*. She *did*. I can't do that if they take me to be fae." He sniffed. "I don't want to be fae. I want to be me."

Crazy elf, I thought. But if there was one thing on this Earth I understood it was emotional turbulence. Calling that turbulence *crazy* never helped anyone.

Hrokr blinked. "So you'll ask?" He must have read my face.

"It's not my decision." It was Ellie's and the cottage's. "Why didn't you ask your father for help?"

Hrokr's eyes narrowed and his belligerent, angry body language resurfaced. "Dad will break my breaking of my concealments," he said. "He'll make it so you can't be bothered to remember me ever again." He hiccupped as if the weight of his loneliness was enough to crush his spine. "I'm sooo boooorrrreeed," he moaned.

How very Loki, I thought.

I grabbed his hand again. "You stay away from Ellie, do you under-stand?" No one hurt my mate. Not Hrokr. Not the fae. Not Arne or Magnus either, for that matter.

Hrokr pouted again.

One of the dryads appeared right next to my bicep. Displaced air rushed over us with an audible pop.

Hrokr screamed. I instinctively tried to swing us away.

She reached out and laid her hand on my elbow. I couldn't move.

The dryad blinked from under her antlered helmet and smiled. "Well, well," she said. "Isn't this interesting."

She reached out her other hand toward someone I could not see. Words I didn't understand fell from her lips.

And we *moved*.

CHAPTER 13

The fae—who was not a mere dryad—grasped the arm of someone on the other side of Hrokr's concealments, and...

I blinked. Hrokr shrieked like a rat skewered to a board. And we were in a pasture, in the snow still, but surrounded by sheep. Big, strong, magically-volatile New Zealand sheep.

About three hundred feet up a small slope, behind the dryad, loomed the massive horse barn of Magnus's compound.

The fae had moved us from the woods between my cabin and the cottage to a field twelve miles outside of town.

"Arne Odinsson!" the dryad bellowed. "Explain this!" She pushed Hrokr away.

She'd brought us to Hrokr's father, or at least close. Me, Hrokr, and... "Ellie?" I yelled. The fae had grabbed someone I couldn't see. Ellie was here. I felt her in the mate dust dancing on my skin.

"Frank!"

I turned around just as Ellie ran up the slope toward us.

She dove into my arms. "I felt other concealments then you disappeared!" She quickly hugged my chest. "Where are we?" She looked around my bicep. "Who are y—*oh, no.*"

The way she said *oh, no* made me want to pick her up and run toward the buildings. She said it as if we'd just stumbled into the David and Goliath situation I dreaded.

Ellie stepped protectively between me and the fae.

The dryad winked and held her finger to her lips.

Ellie inhaled deeply to yell but the dryad whipped a spell that slapped onto Ellie's mouth like a gag. Ellie pawed at the magic, yelling muffled words under the aurora lights dancing on her lips, but nothing coherent came out.

St. Martin had done the same to me under the Samhain blizzard. He'd slapped a shell of magic onto my face and I'd almost suffocated. "Remove the—"

The fae hit me with one, too.

I swiped at my face, growling and yelling under the gag made of shimmering blue and green light. I shouted under the magic.

Ellie stopped pawing at her own gag and grabbed my face. She signaled for me to breathe.

Cold air rushed in through my nostrils but the gag was just a fraction of an inch under my nose. I pawed at it again. Ellie tried to dig her fingers under its edges but the magic was too slippery.

She scooped up a handful of snow and threw it at the fae.

The dryad squinted at me from under her antlered helmet. "Are you panicking, young man?" Her expression shifted into a narrow-eyed, concerned annoyance. "I am not impressed by your lack of fortitude."

She waved her hand and my gag vanished.

I sucked in my breath. I couldn't panic. I wouldn't. What if Ellie couldn't breathe? "Remove Ellie's gag!" I bellowed. "Now!"

The fae shrugged and flicked away Ellie's gag.

She wasn't fuzzing in and out the way the other two dryads had. Her armor didn't carry the same oaken strength as theirs did. It glimmered in the sun as if it carried more air and water than earth and fire.

This fae was pretending to be a dryad.

Confronting any magical with the power to move not only herself but also three other people to a new location would likely get me maimed. Maybe even killed. But this fae smirked, and my breathing was too shallow for me to keep my wits about me. She had gagged my mate.

I lowered my shoulder for a good tackle.

Ellie stopped me. She shook her head and stepped in front of me again.

I looked down at the white pompom on her yellow hat, the set of her cheeks, the fear in her eyes.

Losing me was not going to happen. Not to a blizzard or a gag or a magical with antlers. And certainly not to me allowing the worst of myself to surface.

I pulled her next to me. "Leave us alone," I said to the fae. "Leave Alfheim alone. Hrokr, too. None of this is his fault." I had no idea if that was true, but it certainly felt true.

The fae frowned. "*This* is what got through your concealments, daughter?" She rolled her eyes. "I am *not* impressed."

Daughter? The fae pretending to be an armored-up dryad was an unimpressed Titania?

One thought manifested. One thought that had only a marginal impact on the gravity of the current situation, but if I was honest with myself, would probably have a massive impact on my life—and the lives of everyone around me—on many levels and for a long time to come: *My mother-in-law doesn't like me.*

I locked up. Not for long, but long enough for Titania to catch on to my shock and to manifest a very Loki-like smirk.

"Mom!" Ellie shoved her mother.

Titania danced back from us, laughing as she moved, until she almost tripped over Hrokr.

He blinked and stumbled as if confused and disoriented. He hadn't responded to my yelling, or the gags, though he seemed well aware of the Queen of the Fae.

The concealments must have flipped. I was in Ellie's now and he couldn't see us, though Titania's presence must have manipulated the concealment spells. Thinned them, somehow, since I now could see both Hrokr and Ellie.

He stared at her with a mixture of stone-cold defiance and utter shock.

Then something snapped in that Loki head of his. His lip quivered. He dropped to his knees and wrapped his arms around the neck of a particularly lovely, fluffy white ewe that stood in a small group with two other ewes and a large male lamb.

The four sheep carried ocean-like spirit magic that looked like a spell to keep these domesticated animals away from New Zealand's native wildlife. There was another layer of land magic that wavered in dust and heat, and bubbled as if played on a didgeridoo. Then another layer of elven magic, and a layer of that reminded me of the magic carried by Chip and Lollipop, the two kitsune I'd met in Las Vegas.

This was a breed blessed by the fae, probably long ago, before those of Celtic descent sailed halfway around the world—first to Australia, then on to New Zealand, where the first sheep of the line had been touched by both the kami and the native spirits.

"Save me, Snowdrop, you're my only hope," Hrokr muttered, as if the magic-touched livestock was the only thing standing between him and his vengeful fae family.

The lamb with Snowdrop *baaed* and bounded around Hrokr as if to say, "I'll protect you, Mom!" which just made the scene even more pathetic.

He was messing with Titania. He had to be. No way an elf—any elf, Loki or otherwise—would cower the way he was unless it was part of a distraction plan.

Titania's frown deepened. She, too, didn't seem to believe what she saw. "You shame your mother's memory," she spat.

Hrokr flipped from contrition to attack mode so fast I barely registered his hands forming his spell.

The sigil hit Titania full in the face. She squeaked and jerked, and pawed at it in much the same way I'd pawed at the gag spell.

The antlered helmet tilted. A flare of magic surged upward toward the clouds above and she whipped the spell back at him.

Hrokr spread his arms and took the flashed-back magic full in the chest.

He coughed and buckled over, and for a split second, I swear I saw all the chaos of Loki under his glamour. All the slipperiness and the wanton disregard for everything but his own consuming fire.

Yet he did what he claimed was his true version of his aspect: He'd protected the vulnerable. He'd stepped between the sheep and fae-thrown harm.

Titania turned in a circle and raised her arms. "*O-dins-soooonnnnn!*" she yelled.

Up by the barn, a bubble of magic formed around an opening in the fence as two men walked through side by side, each with their outside hands up as if mirroring each other.

Arne and Magnus pooled their magic in much the same way as the two real dryads had in the woods near my home.

With each step closer, they dropped more of their glamours, and by the time they were halfway to us, their ears stood tall and their ponytails waved behind their heads. They weren't armoring-up, though, and instead manifested finely-woven and intricately-embroidered elven tunics over leather pants and tall, substantial boots.

Arne carried Sal in a scabbard on his back. She touched my mind, but otherwise stayed silent.

Titania threw me a look. Her nose twitched, then she returned her attention to Arne and Magnus.

"Well now, aren't you two superior specimens of elven masculini-ty," Titania drawled.

"Mom!" Ellie snapped. "*What* are you *doing?*"

Titania nodded toward me. The antlers wobbled slightly as if they hadn't quite settled again after Hrokr's magical slap. She grabbed the helmet and a soft, sweet *twing* rang out when her gloves hit the metal. "I came because *he* got through, which is not supposed to happen, daughter." She sniffed. "He's a nice size, though." She winked again. "Lovely in that big-biceped way." She waved dismissively at me. "The tattoos are a bit much."

Hrokr groaned.

She whipped her head and the antlers around again. "And what do

I find when I come for a visit? Is this how you make your mother proud, little Loki boy?"

"Leave him alone, Titania," Arne said as he walked up.

The magic around Arne and Magnus glowed with such brilliance I had to squint. They might be wearing their finest elven fabrics, but they were both on the verge of calling up their armor—and fully dropping their glamours.

That moment at the barn, the moment when Arne went All-Father, it shimmered just out of sight in much the same way as Ellie had when I was inside Hrokr's concealments. Magnus, too. Freyr walked among us in all his terrifying beauty, sexuality, and strength-giving.

They were their gods, Arne and Magnus, not just elves.

Titania didn't seem to care. Or, more precisely, she seemed to expect that they would show her their true faces. She was the Queen of the Fae, after all, and they owed her that respect.

Magnus smoothed the gold and silver stitching on his tunic. "Nice to see you again, Oh Great and Terrible Fae Queen," he said in his best *Hey, beautiful* voice. He grinned and did one of his flirtatious half-winks.

Magnus Freyrsson had just turned a simple, diplomatic greeting into a god-worthy pick-up line.

Titania laughed. "We all cried the day you two left the enclaves of Europe." She nodded her antlers in their direction. "So sorry about your little Christian Ragnarok." She tapped her chin. "Both of them, really. That second one wasn't much fun for us fae, either."

"You know we didn't leave because of the Ragnarok, Titania," Arne said.

"Yes, yes." She shrugged and pointed at Hrokr. "Guess he's not a rumor anymore, is he?"

"I'm sorry, Dad!" Hrokr hugged the poor ewe tighter. "It's not my fault!"

Then he did something I would have kicked him for, if I'd been close enough.

He squared his shoulders and held his head high. "It's Victorsson's fault!" He waved his hand in the general direction of Alfheim. "He invited the fae-born seer into town and now *she's* here." He pointed at Titania.

Ellie gasped but she didn't shrink away. She spread her hand in front of me as if to take the brunt of whatever the elves would have tossed our way if they could see us.

Arne sighed. "Frank had nothing to do with our hidden seer arriving here, Hrokr."

"Well, he broke her concealment enchantments and now grandpa's goons showed up and the seer's mom and—"

"The hidden seer who makes all those extraordinarily useful photographic plates is your *daughter*, Titania?" Arne interrupted.

Titania put her hands on her hips in mock offense. "Would you expect such exquisite work from a mere sprite, Odinsson?"

Magnus grinned. "We only ask because she could have been another sister."

Titania grinned right back at him. "Such a flirtatious elf." The grin turned into a smug smile.

Ellie curled her arms around my waist. "They're going to scare the cottage," she whispered.

If the cottage got too frightened, it would move. Ellie would vanish. I'd lose her. "Will your mother's presence override its need to move?"

She shook her head. "Only if she interferes." She looked up at me. "Mom set the cottage's enchantments. She set the concealments. That's why I can't stop it from moving on my own. I may be the battery but I don't have access to the programming, so to speak. Mom can give it commands. I can't."

The cottage would do what it was meant to do—protect Ellie by moving—unless Titania commanded it not to. "Do you feel its pull?" I asked.

Her brow furrowed. "Only the normal early pulls as evening sets in. We *should* have a couple of hours." She blinked a few times as if she couldn't quite read the signals from the cottage. "But it's tired from last night's work."

"Okay," I said. The mate magic tightened into a swirling veil of sparks around us, making it hard to see Titania and the elves. "What if we run? If we get back to the cottage before sunset?"

She pressed against my front. "It didn't move Chihiro."

Which meant it probably wouldn't move me.

Arne opened his arms wide. "I hereby welcome our seer to Alfheim." He stared directly at the Queen. "As King of this enclave, I officially extend the protections of Alfheim to the fae-born witch daughter of Queen Titania." He continued to stare at her. "We will not interfere with her concealment enchantments and trust Frank Victorsson to continue interfacing for us."

Ellie squeezed my hand.

Arne nodded toward Titania. "Satisfied?"

All sound stopped. No wind. No rustling or murmurs from the barns. No chittering or chirping, either.

Titania sighed. "It doesn't matter, Odinsson. You have been hiding my stepdaughter's son from his grandfather. You and I both know this cannot stand."

Stepdaughter's son... Arne's fae princess... Gotland... *She was all things feminine...*

None of Arne and Magnus's animosity had been about Ellie. It had all been about Hrokr.

Magnus twitched. He flicked his hands and a sigil appeared between Hrokr and Titania. Another appeared in front of Arne and Magnus.

"It would be best if you left now, Titania," Magnus said. "No harm. No foul. We will handle Oberon's sentinels on our own."

Her laughter filled the pasture and the four sheep *baaed* in response. "Oh, you sweet, sweet, handsome elf man." She threw wide her arms. "The moment he figures out you've been hiding his grandson from him, he's going to hex your crops, steal your daughters, and buy up your little town so he can mow it under. You know that."

Neither Arne nor Magnus moved, nor did the sigils.

"Why do you think *I'm* here, Titania?" Magnus asked.

He could have taken half of Alfheim's elves and started a second North American enclave long ago. He could have moved down to The Cities and become the founder of several great Minnesota industries.

Magnus Freyrsson stayed in Alfheim because the best protection for the entire Upper Midwest against an angry, hex-throwing Fae King was an equally terrifying Freyr aspect elf.

Arne and Magnus had just shown Titania that they had a tool the fae did not—they worked together. The enclaves had their politics, but the world's elves would come if Arne called.

They would come for their Odin elves. So would the werewolves. As would I. And now Ellie, too. So who was the true King here?

Arne grinned. "Your daughter lives with us now," he said. "This is your fight, too."

He'd back her, if she asked. If he could trust her. If she, too, would come when he called.

Her posture shifted. She was thinking about what a fae war would mean, and what it might cost her to become the Fae Empress.

Her shoulders dropped ever so slightly as if the weight of the unspoken words between these moments had fully landed on her person.

She might act a trickster, and bully Hrokr and her own daughter, but she was Queen, and as such, such grand schemes must be fully considered. Rashness is what got you dethroned.

The defiant anger returned.

There was no way we'd get to the cottage in time if she forced a move. None at all. I coiled my hands under Ellie's backpack to hold her as closely as I could.

"No, she doesn't, Odinsson," Titania said. "The boy, neither. He's fae. He comes with me."

"Leave me alone!" Hrokr yelled.

Arne blinked. The Loki man-child whose power rippled around him with almost as much strength as his father's, the problem child Arne had hidden all these years, was about to be ripped away from his father in much the same way as Ellie was about to be ripped from me.

Taken. Kidnapped. And most likely lost forever to the fog of fae-generated concealment enchantments.

I picked up Ellie and set her behind me. She squeaked, but didn't argue, and pressed herself against my back.

Titania laughed. "Aren't you gallant." She nodded to Arne. "The big semi-dead ones make good paladins, do they not?"

His eyes rounded. He'd just realized I must be here along with Titania's daughter. But the concealments made the realization vanish as quickly as it appeared.

Titania chuckled. "I built your concealments to last, Ellie my girl." She pointed at Arne as if he was the root of all the troubles that caused her to set the spells. "They've kept you safe all these years."

"I'm safe *here*, mother!" Ellie gripped my arm. "With Frank. With these elves. There's a pack here, too. A large, strong pack with three Alphas. I want to stay."

Titania shook her head and her antlers tilted again. "I will take you home. The cottage will do as I tell it and follow. From there, it can take you someplace safe from elves."

"It likes Frank. It wants to stay here, too!" Ellie said.

In the shadow of her helmet, Titania's eyes physically brightened as if her magic had burned through her skull into the mundane world. "We'll see about that."

Arne's magic pulsed. "Let us talk this through." He tightened his sigils. Salvation, from his back, threw out her own wall of magic to supplement his, and he took a step toward Titania.

"Tell that blade to *be quiet*," Titania snapped. "Do not bring more ills into this moment! It's bad enough you brought it to this meeting."

Sal again receded into the background.

"Come up to the barn," Magnus said seductively. "Visit the horses. We can ride together through the snow."

Titania balled her hands into fists. "Your stallions are *not* a fair trade, Magnus Freyrsson. Not for my daughter's life." She hit him with a bolt of searing magic so bright we all cringed.

Magnus staggered. He gasped. He did not fall.

His sigils did.

A rope of magic flew from Titania's hand and coiled around Hrokr. He screeched, and one of her gags followed.

Another rope coiled by my side.

I didn't think. I reacted. I sunk both of my hands into the snake of fae magic reaching for Ellie. I grasped. I shook. I needed to get it to turn away.

It didn't. It bit.

The dusting mate magic around my hands sucked away into Titania's magic. It pulled off me, away from my skin, and off my soul. Only a hole remained where connection should have been.

She still held tight to my waist. She still breathed against my arm. I heard her cries and smelled the salt of her tears, but my soul thought it nothing more than memories.

Like the dryads, Ellie was lost in an illusion of distance I could not understand.

"Mother!" she yelled. "Let him *go!*"

Titania looked at her hand as if she, too, saw her dreadful snake and the mate magic it consumed. Her lips rounded. *"Huh,"* she said.

"You dare hunt on my lands?" Arne reached over his shoulder to draw Sal.

Titania pointed at him. "Do you want a war, Odinsson? If an Odin aspect uses that axe against a fae you know damned well *all* fae will descend on your little fiefdom."

Arne held Sal's handle but did not lift her off his back. "Leave, Titania. Alone."

"And what?" she asked. "Be strategic? Make plans? Operate under the rules of the game?" She thrust out her chin. "Rules do not apply to my husband." She looked back at us. "I can't leave you with them," she said. "I can't have his wrath fall on you."

Arne's eyes widened in surprise as if he realized once again that Ellie had to be here—which meant he probably realized once more that I was here, also.

Hrokr struggled against his rope, but it did no good. *"No no no..."* he whimpered through the gag.

"Mom!" Ellie shrieked. "Don't!"

Titania raised her hands to the sky as if to call down the clouds themselves, and... the magic shifted. The fae magic. The elven magic. All the residual kami and spirit magic around the sheep. It all took on the same red and green, feral energy of the cottage. The same sense of living under understanding I'd been given in the lucid dream I'd had last night. The one where the *other* magic wanted me to learn.

To be aware.

But I had no way of doing so. No way to hook into *any* magic no matter its origins, because I was not myself magical.

I was reconstituted and mundane. I was more science than art. And Ellie was about to be yanked from me forever.

She gulped and held tighter to my waist. "If you do this, I will never forgive you, Mom. *Never.*"

"I'll go with her!" I yelled. Maybe Titania would listen. Maybe she'd send me, too.

I knew what the hole was. Each individual part of me had been inside it before my father's brew of chemistry and power had jolted my stitched-together body to life. I'd walked inside it in The Land of the Dead. I'd stared it down when I lost Rose.

If Titania stole Ellie from me, maybe I'd remember. Or maybe the enchantments would reestablish and I'd forget. But the hole, the loss, the black depth draining away my soul would never leave.

It would roil underneath, unfettered and feral.

Titania cocked her head until her antlers touched her shoulder. "My husband will smell the elves on you, young man."

She threw her arms wide.

The sigil's around Arne's hands brightened. "You can fix this, son," he said.

His words were meant for Hrokr. I was sure they were meant for Hrokr, because Hrokr was his son with the magic. Yet Arne looked at *me*.

I didn't have time for my screaming raccoon, nor did I have time for Hrokr's menagerie of biting and hissing internal ferals, but they were all here with us anyway. The Loki elf and I were the princesses at the center of our own very special circle of dancing forest creatures, and ours weren't going to clean anyone's house.

I looked to Hrokr. "You protect the vulnerable," I said. He'd done it before. He could do it again, even coiled in Titania's magic rope.

And Ellie Jones, my half-fae mate, backpack on her back and Maura's silly bright yellow knit hat with the huge white pompom on her head, clung to my side as if this really was the end of the world.

Ellie's cottage—the magic of the cottage—had tried to teach me that we were all part of the same universe, the same magical ecosystem. We were all interlaced. Some parts were more local than others, but no part held more importance, even the old, old parts that cared nothing for humanity or its magicals.

The land answered the two dryads' calls. The trees mapped space and time. They sheltered their skittering things, and they held firm to this world.

So the trees did what they should not have been able to do. Maybe they responded to the presence of the fae. Or the angry elves. Or perhaps they noticed the layers of overlapping concealment enchantments. Or maybe, just maybe, the old parts under all magic responded.

The King and Queen of the Fae weren't the only non-elven magicals to take notice.

And no one wanted this to end in the ash and hell of yet another Ragnarok.

Hrokr's hands flickered. He added *something* to his father's sigils.

I wrapped myself around Ellie. *Please help*, I whispered into the ether, to the other magic. To the other pantheons who had taken notice while I was in St. Martin's bubble with Axlam and Dagrun. To Raven, too, if she cared to listen.

Please don't open this wound. *Please.*

Branches reached. Portals snared. My Yggdrasil tattoo felt as if it uprooted from my skin. And we *moved*, all us emotional racoons, menageries, and angry All-Fathers.

We moved someplace just across a border from Alfheim, Minnesota.

CHAPTER 14

I enlisted in the Fifth Minnesota Volunteer Infantry Regiment on the third day of April, 1862. We fought many battles, mostly in Mississippi and Louisiana. I wasn't part of the First, the men who took the Twenty-eighth Virginia's battle flag at Gettysburg, so I don't have that glory. I was at the Battle of Nashville, though.

I remember the stench of decay in the hot soupy air. The dysentery and the malaria. The screams and the moans and the horror of weaponized death.

And I remember how a fae responded.

Self-sustaining magicals—elves, fae, kami, any of the other groups —they're all basically the same species. Of all the subspecies out there, the elves are the most homogeneous—and the most human. They're Norse gifted power by their gods.

But the fae, they vary. Some are like Ellie and her mother—more *homo sapiens* than *homo mageía*. Some are closer to the wolf part of the World Wolf, or the stag part of the World Stag. Some are as much manifestation as they are conscious creatures.

The American Civil War mortally wounded not only men, but also the land. The magic where battles were fought was now bloated and bruised. To this day, many places still suffer a form of gangrene.

And that one fae, that one Tennessee night, manifested out of the fog. He stood on his stag legs under the bitter moon and he swung razor-sharp antlers. He cut out the infection as best he could.

My best guess was that he'd come to America with the Scots-Irish who inhabited Appalachia. Or perhaps the French. Or perhaps he was as old as the forest itself—all forests everywhere—and had come through from a fae realm to do the regiments damage. I did not know. I know only that he wasn't a Native spirit. He was one-hundred-percent-antigen fae.

Four-toed undulate feet scraped through the rich soil. Deep stag calls rolled through the fog. The night went cold and men died in ways mundanes could not fathom. Ways that would the next day be attributed to cannons and bayonets. To war and pestilence.

So I understood what fae were capable of. What a kami or a loa or a spirit could render. What elves could inflict, if they chose to do so. How a barrier could be ripped asunder as a warning. How things that should not come through, can.

Or things that should not be allowed in, are.

As magic snatched not only me, but also Sal, Ellie, Titania, and the elves, I felt the barrier's agony. Not the suffering of what crosses, but the white-hot screaming of the magic itself.

The agony of Ellie's cottage when it moves. The sweltering sting caused when a pocketland is cut off from the world and made a realm. The strained fibers, both the real and the magical, that hold the universe together.

What came of this? Rage burning outward from a gushing wound. The need to ride, and to break, and to inflict as a way to spend that pain.

Crossing into The Great Hall never hurt like this. Neither did crossing into The Land of the Dead. This magic, this elemental truth of the fae, set every living part of my body on fire.

Then it all froze.

~

I STILL STOOD in the snow, in the pasture, under the knoll and away from Magnus's barns, but this place was different.

I was in the world, but not the real world. I was pretty sure that whatever Hrokr had done, whatever extra call he'd pushed out with his additions to his father's magic, had shunted me at least—all of us, maybe—into a reflection.

Nothing made sense, though everything did. Left was right, and right was left, except I was not flipped, and my dominant hand still wanted to do the throwing and the hitting. Nothing looked mirrored, but I knew my senses were not operating correctly.

Time was not working correctly.

Titania's ropes of magic coiled around Ellie and Hrokr. They also coiled up her arms and over her shoulders, where they coiled around her neck, face, and up under her antlered helmet. The ropes pulsed and rippled like water, or gel, but Titania, Hrokr, and Ellie stood frozen as if between film frames.

"Ellie?" My voice echoed as if someone had added reverb, or as if I called from a long way off and my words bounced off Magnus's barns.

That reverb hit the hole left behind after Titania's magic sucked away my mate magic.

Resonance isn't a term usually associated with the chaos of anger. The thing is, anger and rage aren't as chaotic as humans would like to believe. Chaos gives cover. "I was so angry I couldn't foresee the outcomes of my actions" type of cover.

But that's a lie. Anger and rage aren't chaos. They're a rupture. They represent a living thing's cataclysmic response to what it sees as overwhelming opposition. It's a raccoon backed against a shed, or me roaring promised vengeance at my father.

The outcome of such episodes is always, always predictable.

And here I was, fully aware that this place was not right, that time here was *not right*, that I was in an illusion and facing the loss of the first woman in my more-than-two-hundred-year life who loved me unconditionally.

I could wait for all the conditions that might possibly cause her to walk away, but they weren't there. They never would be.

Unless the rage took me again.

The rage.

It's not chaos. It's not. It's resonance inside a hole, and whatever this place was rang that stupid, still-there, always-*there*, bell.

And I had to fight back. I had to rupture what attacked so I could escape through the rip. I had no choice.

I had to swing my razor-sharp antlers and cut out the infection.

The sigils between the elves and Titania pulsed and wiggled as much as the ropes of fae magic. Arne and Magnus, also frozen, gleamed so brightly behind their glamours they looked to be in the first nanosecond of an explosion.

But not Sal. She was here with me in this bubble of time, and she, too, felt the resonance.

Battle roared from her in a breathtaking wave as resonant as my own echoes.

I dodged the ropes. I swung around the sigils. And I lifted my axe from King Odinsson's back.

Mine roared out after *battle*. I had returned for her. I belonged to *her*.

Every rune on her blade glowed like the sun itself. The violet-colored magic that allowed me to wield her buzzed as if it was about to transcend into ultraviolet. My axe knew her purpose and she would avenge those in need of vengeance. She was the blazing blade of Salvation, brought forth with her sister sword from Nidavellir and forged in the fires of Mount Eldgjá. She cut a path through those who claimed righteousness but who brought only death and destruction.

I twirled her around my wrist and she sang her glory to the universe.

We would stand between our own and any Ragnarok, great or small, vampire or wolf. Fae or mundane. We were rage harnessed.

I dodged around Arne's frozen sigil, arm up, and ready to slice through limbs and magic. Fae limbs. Arms and legs and neck of a royal who threatened my family. My mate.

Sal and I would sever these tentacles that threatened our elves and we would slaughter any who—

Slaughter.

One of the ewes *baaed.* She lifted her head high and she called into the magic that was this place. She touched the truth. She called out all that roamed inside this mirror place.

And she would not allow me to forget who I was.

I do not kill. I have *never* murdered. I would not kill. Even at my weakest, I understood not to cause irreparable harm. I would not cause someone else to become how I had been.

"No!" I dropped Sal. Again. I dropped her to the snow and I stepped back. "We can't." There'd be a cataclysm. A war.

Ragnarok. And I'd lose everything and everyone yet again.

I glanced at frozen Hrokr. It was supposed to be a thorn that precipitated the end times, not a lone Loki elf trying to help.

No one moved but the sheep. We were in the shadow lands, the place of twilight where Midgard bumped up against all the other realms. Ivan and Dracula had formed Vampland from the raw material here. All realms budded off the real world through this material, like little universes pushing though into their own regions of space and time.

We weren't *in* a bubble. We were *on* a bubble. We were *inside* the veil itself. We were in a magical event horizon.

Hrokr had stopped us from moving into Titania's realm, or any fae realm, and had accidentally allowed the mirror of this place to magnify my rage into flashing life inside my personal resonance chamber.

I had to get out of here. I had to, or the rage would take over again. I rubbed my temple and looked around. How was I supposed to get Ellie out of her mother's magical grip?

"We do one killing," Sal said. "We kill the spell."

I looked down at her glowing runes and her ultraviolet handle. She spoke in a real, actual voice, or at least a voice that was real as this place allowed. She somehow modulated the air to make words that could be heard.

That voice had carried Dagrun-level authority.

"No killing, Salvation," I said.

My father had framed me for several murders. I had my reasons for hating him. Legitimate reasons. He left stories and documents out in the world that, to this day, describe me as an eight-foot monster full of self-centered and self-absorbed pain and rage. He was the killer, not me.

If I killed, there'd be consequences. There were always consequences. Because the darkness might be a hole but it was never alone. It came with prison walls.

"Disrupt, then," Sal said. "You can get the helpful fae magic away before the Queen comes fully through."

"You're helping now?" I asked.

Her runes pulsed. "Our King believes the fae magic to be of value."

So Salvation helped for Arne's sake, not mine.

I'd take what I could get. "We're inside the veil itself."

"We're in the switching station," Sal said. "We're standing in the map. Once they're here, they will realize their spells need rerouting. In here, that's easy."

My axe had the voice of an opera singer, or a goddess. One a person did not disobey.

If I got Ellie to the cottage before Titania realized what we were doing, the cottage would control where Ellie moved to, not her mother. I'd have a higher chance of remembering her after the fact— and figuring out where it took her.

Which meant I could find her.

"Are you going to do another deep dive into jealousy if we do this?" Because I'd find another way if I had even the slightest inkling that my axe might hurt Ellie.

Sal seemed surprised that I still cared so much, since my mate magic had disappeared.

A blip of rage blanked out my senses. There was no seeing Titania, or the elves, or Sal. No smelling the crystal-clear air here. No thought of consequences.

I almost snapped Sal's handle in half.

She yipped and I caught myself. This place removed any and all moderation. It distilled, and when one of its modulated waves crashed into me, it *crashed*.

I dropped Sal yet again.

There was no chaos here, only rage looking for chaotic cover. I had to remember that. Breathe it. Feel it in place of my lost mate magic.

Sal's warrior needs were not helping.

I shook my head and took a step toward Magnus. "Maybe the elves are carrying something that will work."

"Wait!" Sal said. "Love isn't only mate magic." Her voice *resonated*.

"I don't think you should be talking, Sal," I said.

Swing me wide and I will disrupt the tentacle, she pushed into my head. *I must warn you: It will hurt.* "I will be unconscious for some time afterward," she said.

If it would knock her unconscious, it meant snapping the tentacle would release a lot of energy. What about Arne and Magnus? "Will this hurt the elves?"

She paused. *Our King and his Second can take care of themselves,* she thought-said. She paused again. *They will process this place in a way not unlike how you were—are—responding.*

Raging elves and a raging Queen of the Fae. Not a good mix.

Suddenly, as if a motor had engaged, the sigils ground into the snow and dirt like two massive saw blades, doing at least three full spins in a blink of an eye before freezing again.

I jumped back.

"They've almost settled onto the surface of this bubble," Sal said.

I snatched her off the ground and spun toward the magical rope rippling around Ellie. "Deep breath, my friend."

Sal did her version of an inhale.

I slammed her blade into Titania's magic.

CHAPTER 15

To rupture is to tear violently without control. Something you wanted contained always comes gushing forth. There's no way around the spilling of guts.

The thing with real ruptures is that they don't mend themselves. Even after all the pain and anger spills from the wound, that hole in the soul is still there. Which is why I'm thankful my mind was never as piecemeal as my body. If it had been, the rips and the agony would have needed surgery to fix. And no one can be their own surgeon.

My brushes with tearing have made me that much more sensitive to magic. I can see if magic is stable, precarious, agitated, or about to burst. I can read the spits and the sparks and the vibrating sheets. I know good magic from bad, and good magic going bad.

But nothing had prepared me for the magical rupture I caused when I sliced through Titania's snake-ropes of power.

The moment Sal's blade touched the outer edge of the rope, I felt the magic reverberate through her metal, into her handle, and up the woven magic around her grip.

A reverb similar to, yet different from, the same oscillating waves that had rung through the space of the veil earlier. It felt deeper this time. Lower, as if the entire boundary vibrated.

Sal slipped through the magic as if she were slicing off bits of gelatin which didn't give the resistance I expected. I stumbled into the wound as Sal's head slammed into the snow-covered pasture and for an instant—a microsecond blink of an eye—I was connected to Titania's magic.

Red and green. Tooth and claw. Hunger and sex and warm bones. Fae magic was alive and free and only cooperated because a fae it liked fed it good treats and kept its cubs warm and safe.

And now I'd sliced open that magic, and it spilled so violently it slammed me backward into Arne's ready-to-buzz sigil.

My back hit what felt like a vertical puddle of acid. When Sal's handle hit the sigil, my arm went numb.

She was unconscious, as she warned she'd be. She couldn't help. I leaned forward, trying to get off Arne's barrier, as I willed my numb hand and fingers to not let go.

The shield sigil spun once, twice, three times—and spun my perception with it. I didn't move—my body stayed against the magic Arne had raised to shield himself from Titania—but my sense of the boundary flashed forward, then back, then forward again as if the ground itself flipped. My perspective flipped from snow-covered and elven to richly green and fae and back again.

The elves, my home, the magic of Alfheim, the steady state of the region's Norse heritage, the calm of so-called Minnesota Nice, the predictability of snowfall and snowplows, the cycle of freeze and thaw of my lake—these were quiet waves. Order and chaos balanced. No ruptures. No gushing.

But Titania—and all the fae—were all about the peaks and the valleys. All about the emotions and touches and worship of nature's wonders. Entire realms were built around perfect apples. Religions manifested out of the fervor and raucous dances under Beltane moons. And chaos balanced order.

Then back to Arne and Magnus. Back to the riotous democratic—yet controlled—violence of the Norse gods.

Then Titania and the layers and layers of festivals and goddesses worshiped.

My gut rolled. A pounding throb smashed against my temples and if I didn't get off Arne's sawblade, I'd lose myself in the back and forth flashes. I'd be vulnerable.

Titania might take Ellie again and the acid-like pain, all the reverberations and the echoes and the veil-rupturing magic, would be my life, or lack of life. Lack of mate magic. Lack of reason and emotion and the brilliant wonder that was Ellie, half-asleep and skin-to-skin, under the warm golden sun of her cottage.

Ellie, also alone, somewhere she couldn't leave, not knowing if I remembered her and probably stripped of her own memories of me.

I bellowed but my yell came right back at me, like all things in this mirror-thin place between worlds, and hit me full force with its teeth and claws.

I gasped to pull in what breath I could. I'd survived a pike through my chest. I was not going to my end because I'd accidentally backed into an elf's sigil. I wouldn't be collateral damage in something so banal.

A shadow appeared in front of me. Two hands reached through the wavering mirror-like waves and pulled me away from Arne's sigil.

"Frank!" Hrokr Arnesson peered at my face, then around my arm at his father's sigil. "Move!"

He tossed me, Sal still in my hand, toward Ellie.

I stumbled, but managed to avoid Titania, and somehow circumvented her flailing, sparking magic before falling to my knees in front of Ellie.

Sal had said nothing about possible ill effects on Ellie and Hrokr from rupturing Titania's magic. No mention of how it would stun Ellie into incoherence, or cause Hrokr to change.

I looked back at the Loki elf.

There was concern there, in that face, hidden amongst the burning awe.

I shouldn't have looked at Arne when he went All-Father back at the barn. I shouldn't look at Hrokr now. One should not look upon the face of a god.

Hrokr Arnesson's ears were no longer the same tall, pointy shape of the elves, and had lost a good three inches as they rounded down into something more sprite-like. A subtle rainbow of colors now danced in his gray elven ponytail and in the sparks of magic outlining every single tattoo on his face, scalp, and neck. His clothes had changed from the black hunting leathers into tighter-fitting, strapped-down, somehow darker-than-black fighting gear. He was now fully covered from the collar around his neck to his gloved hands and his massive, knee-covering boots.

Fire spat and slapped in his magic. The control of his elven sigils had given way to that slippery, burning truth that had always been underneath.

But it was his eyes that frightened me the most.

The concealed elf, the man whose father had hidden him not only from Alfheim, but from the fae, stood in front of me with eyes as utterly black as his clothes. Eyes that held the cosmos, and eyes that stole souls. Magic flickered out the sides of those eyes as if his vision was on fire.

The witch in the bayou, the one from whom I took Rose, had eyes like that. She'd stared off into her own raw, uncontrolled power. Rose had too, at the end.

Hrokr whipped up a counter sigil to slow his father's grinding shield. He glanced toward his father. "I'm sorry, Dad. I was trying to divert her magic."

I touched Ellie's arm. "Honey?"

She blinked. A retch-like shudder spasmed through her body. "Mom's magic…"

"I severed the ropes." I helped her to her feet. "So she couldn't pull you into her realm."

She looked up and to the southeast. "The cottage…" Her entire body shivered. "It's terrified. It can't quite feel me. It doesn't know what to do."

"Is it pulling you back? Is it trying to move?" If it was only pulling her back, then she'd be safe. But it moved, too…

Ellie continued to stare southeast. "Sal cut the routing magic?"

"Yes," I said. How long would Titania and the elves be frozen?

"Arne and Magnus can get us back to Alfheim." If they realized we were between realms. If they didn't fall to the oscillations.

She rubbed her arms. "We need to get out of here." She leaned against me, and magical sparks flew when her backpack knocked against Sal's handle. "Mom is caught here." She shivered again, but this time I was sure it was more out of terror than chill. "She'll be in pain when she's fully through, and driven to reconnect to the correct pathways."

I'd hurt Titania when I slashed her connection to Ellie and Hrokr. I'd caused her pain and disorientation and now we were stuck inside the veil with the most powerful, soon to be the most vengeful, of the fae.

And two also-disoriented elder elves whose power levels I understood intellectually, but had only seen peripherally.

Hrokr whipped up another sigil, this between him and Titania. "She'll hunt," he said.

Ellie tugged on my hand. "We need to get to the cottage. It will protect us."

She meant the cottage would protect her. I was the one who had done this. I doubted it would protect me from Titania's rage.

"It's going to move, Frank," she said. "If it moves me without Mom interfering, we'll..." She looked up at me. "We'll be able to find each other. I'll remember you. You'll remember, like Chihiro. We'll find each other."

Her face said she didn't believe her own words. "I'll find you. I promise," I said.

Ellie bit her lip and hugged me tightly. "I know."

Hrokr cleared his throat. "This place shifts," he said. "You might make it. Or you might end up purifying yourself in the waters of Lake Minnetonka."

Ellie looked down at the ground and slowly nodded her head. "Okay," she said. "Okay." She looked up at me. "We have to try."

She wasn't giving up. She looked back at Hrokr. "Come with us."

The fire streaming from the sides of his cosmos-eyes blazed with all the glory of his god. "Are you offering me shelter inside your concealments?" he asked.

Ellie must have realized what she'd just done. "I am offering you an audience at my gate to state your case."

He'd wanted to know if Ellie would protect him, too. Now he had his answer. He bowed his head. "Go!" He turned back to his father, but thought better of it. "Take my sheep," he said.

The *or else* in his voice rode out on a wave of slippery, fiery magic and dripped between us—unspoken yet just as destructive as a splash of acid.

Ellie sucked in her breath. "*Loki*," she breathed.

"Yes," Hrokr said.

Tension hardened her face and neck. "Do not attempt to trick my mother, Loki elf," she said. "She will chew you up and spit you out."

If he heard her, much less understood, I could not tell. He pointed at the sheep again. "Snowdrop," he said.

Hrokr turned his back to us.

We needed a way to get to the cottage. "Will we find vehicles here?" I pointed at the barn. Anything that might help us make the twelve miles back to the cottage before the cottage closed up for the night.

"I don't know," Ellie said.

I scooped the lamb up in my arms as we ran up the hill, hoping for one small bit of luck.

CHAPTER 16

We were between realms, in the fabric of the veil itself, in the in-between where magic influenced the real world. We were quite literally inside the geometric lock that opened and closed contact between The Land of the Living and all the other Lands, Dead or otherwise.

I had my doubts about access to combustion engines here, or either of the elves' lovely electric vehicles. This was not a plane where mundane science worked.

We had to try anyway.

With Sal on one shoulder and the lamb tucked under my other arm, I followed Ellie and the three ewes up the hill. A bonfire of magic blazed behind us, a tortured mix of fae chaos and streamlined elven spells. Hrokr stood in the center, between his father and his step-grandmother, adding—or subtracting, I couldn't tell. He disrupted, for sure.

Perhaps leaving the Loki elf in the center of what might just turn into the magical equivalent of an international incident wasn't the best idea.

Not one moment of this had been a good idea. Not my misinterpreting Arne's concern about Hrokr as a threat to Ellie. Not my mishandling the dryads, because I was pretty sure I mishandled that situation, even if I didn't know how. Not in how I responded to Hrokr and his requests. Or his threats.

Or fully trusting Sal when she said to cut the magic ropes.

She was still unconscious. Had she realized that her slice would harm Titania? And that the harm would cause even worse problems? Did she care? *Battle* was her focus, so *battle* we did. When one's only tool is an axe, one does a lot of chopping and splitting.

What other choice did we have? Without Sal disrupting the entire magical circuit, Ellie would be gone, and Oberon would likely show up looking for his grandson.

Which at this point was probably inevitable, considering the blazing, blinding magic erupting from the wound I'd caused.

And my girlfriend's mother, the Queen of the Fae, was about to hunt for us, and the elves, and probably everything else here in the veil. Hunt me as if I was some idiot village boy whom she'd decided was not at all worthy of her daughter.

The three ewes ducked under the fence just as a flash and a magical concussive wave hit our backs.

Ellie stumbled. The lamb jumped from my arm and followed his mother under the fence, and I accidently dropped Sal while juggling her and the animal.

She hit the snow with a yelp and a sudden, utter re-awakening into consciousness.

She swore in what sounded like Old Norse.

Ellie pointed at my axe. "Did she just talk?"

"The helpful fae magic is close by?" Sal said. "Freeing her worked?"

Ellie scrambled to her feet. "We need to go." She turned toward the fence.

I reached for Sal. My reach required a twist, and I caught a glimpse of the magical storm behind us.

Titania's ruptured magic gelled around her body. The antlered helmet sharpened into a rack of obsidian knives. The borrowed dryad armor solidified into sections of cutting light that appeared to float above her skin.

"How *dare* you!" she roared, and sent a thick, massive bolt against the elves' sigils just as Arne and Magnus snapped through the barrier into the semi-realm of the veil, both in full armor, but without weapons. They were, it seemed, adhering to whatever treaty or promise they'd made to not bring along elven artifacts.

"Don't let the fae steal me," Sal said.

I picked her up, wishing for Arne's scabbard, and set her on my shoulder. "I won't," I said.

Arne whipped out a new shield, but at an angle to the ground—an angle good for running and launching an attack.

Magnus bolted up the ramp and dove for Titania. Her hands came up to zap him, but he grabbed her and they rolled across the snowy pasture, armor clinking and clacking, until Titania's razor antlers caught the ground.

She punched the side of Magnus's head. He hollered and rolled into a crouch.

Titania jumped to her own crouch. "Why do the pretty ones always put up the worst fights?" She kicked Magnus away.

Arne motioned to Hrokr to come over to him. The Loki elf looked first at his father, then at Titania and Magnus. Then he looked at us.

The fire magic around his eyes flared. He smiled.

Behind us, a horse snorted.

"Whoa whoa *whoa!*" Ellie yelled.

I looked back at the fence. Bloodyhoof stood on the other side of the fence's wooden rails, his handsome bay coat shimmering a deep red and his black-filled Fjord-horse mane brushed up and standing on end as if he was the greatest of Greek war horses.

He wasn't Greek. He was Norse, and he was not going to allow the Fae Queen to attack his elves.

"I'd forgotten that he's as beautiful as Magnus," Ellie breathed.

The stallion's eyes blazed in much the same way they had while we were in Vampland, except this time, the fire looked more alive. More chaotic. More… Loki.

I looked back at Hrokr. He'd somehow done this.

Bloodyhoof whinnied and pawed at the ground. He pranced to the side just as the lamb darted between his hooves.

"Blodughofi is drawn to the hunt," Sal said.

The stallion raised his head and *neighed* out a call. Two other horses responded.

Lucky and Comet, the two Percherons stolen by Tony and Ivan and forced into Vampland, thundered around the side of the barn and leaped the fence as if they were show jumpers.

"Hrokr sent the sheep into the barn," I said. He must have used them to bring out the horses.

I held out my hand as I scooped up Sal with my other. "Blodughofi, my friend," I said. "How about we ride you out of here?"

Bloodyhoof snorted again. He sniffed at Ellie, then backed up.

"If he jumps here, he'll land on—"

The stallion leaped. He arched his grand back and he pushed off the ground with all the strength of his powerful hindquarters.

Bloodyhoof sailed over the fence, and us, as if he could fly.

"Oh… oh *wow*," Ellie said. "He's worthy of a valkyrie."

The last magical I wanted to see right now was a valkyrie. "We need to go. Magnus has other horses." Maybe we'd get lucky and a more rideable animal would come through.

Arne and Magnus's sigils parted with an audible pop and opened just enough of a rip for Bloodyhoof to jump through. He landed to the side of Titania and reared up as if to stomp her into the muddy snow.

She roared and jumped back, her hands coming up to hit Bloody-hoof with a bolt.

The two Percherons charged in, both kicking at the Queen, and keeping her from striking the stallion with magic.

"Magnus needs to get those horses away from her." Ellie curled her arms around my waist. "If she hurts them…"

If she hurt Magnus's prize horses, there'd be a war, but Ellie's face said something else—there'd be trauma. Not just to the horses, or the elves, but to Titania, too. Hurting beasts would trigger a new cascade of anguish that would make any war that much worse.

There was nothing we could do. The horses circled. Magnus tried to calm Titania. And Arne held out his hands to his son.

Hrokr looked at his father. He looked at the horses circling Titania. Then he looked directly at Ellie and me.

Something shifted again. Something slippery and both planned yet heavily dependent on the moment. Something utterly trickster.

Hrokr darted for Bloodyhoof. He was up on the stallion's back with his hands curled in the horse's mane before the other magicals could respond.

Arne yelled his son's name. Angry magic flared around Magnus. And Titania saw her opening.

She sidestepped and swung her arm in a wide circle. All the crystalline magic of her armor and antlered helmet, all the icy colors and the sharp facets, swung with her arm.

She opened a portal.

The first horse that jumped through ran straight at Bloodyhoof. The second ran at Arne. The third at Magnus. The fourth toward the Percherons. The fifth Titania mounted.

The sixth ran up the hill toward Ellie and me.

This stallion was a tall, willowy creature with a sleek greenish-champagne coat. A bridle of silver and gold gleamed around his muzzle. A shroud followed behind the beast like the gossamer sheets of a specter, and he was too thin, too skeletal, to be a true horse.

Titania had called up nightmares. Death horses.

Ellie looked at the barn, then back at the ghost horses circling Magnus's three.

The horses snorted. They whinnied and reared and pawed at each other like fighting mustangs. The elves shot bolts at Titania, who sent them right back.

I twisted Ellie behind me and pulled us out of the way of the charging stallion. He slowed, but not fast enough, and jumped the fence to keep from running into it.

We couldn't go to the barns. We couldn't go toward the fight.

Ellie grabbed my hand and pulled me west along the fence, toward the other buildings. "This way," she said.

Hrokr, all his self-disappointment dancing across his god-face, looked at us from Bloodyhoof's back. Alfheim's Loki elf had unleashed something he hadn't meant to unleash. He'd tried to be better, to tame his chaos, but Loki is what Loki does.

And he might get his father killed.

How long could they fight like this? How long before the other elves noticed? Or Oberon? Ellie was right; we had to get out of here. I followed her along the fence.

"Our King will prevail." Sal said it as if she carried no doubt about Arne's fighting capability.

I wasn't worried about Arne and Magnus, or Titania, either. I was worried about Hrokr. About his responses to all this. And about other fae showing up.

We had a twelve-mile trip back to the lake as the crow flies, and we needed to make it before the cottage closed up for the night. If we couldn't find another horse enchanted enough to cross into the veil, we'd have to run it. I could, but I wasn't sure about Ellie.

Hrokr leaned toward Bloodyhoof's ear. A bit of magic moved from the elf to the horse. And Magnus's prize stallion reared up one last time and broke east, away from us and the fight.

"Hrokr!" Arne's magic flared up toward the sky as he watched his son ride away.

Magnus's magic also flared.

"Enough!" Arne bellowed.

The flash that followed hit the ghost horses menacing the Percherons. It hit the one menacing us as it turned to jump back over the fence. It hit the two harassing Arne and Magnus.

All the ghost horses vanished. All except the one Titania rode.

The hit from Arne's magic almost knocked her off the back of the horse. She righted herself quickly, rolling up into a squat as her ghost stallion circled.

She turned toward us. Her hand rose. She pointed.

Her ghost stallion charged up the hill.

"*No no no!*" Ellie sprinted along the fence. There had to be a place for her to hide. There had to be.

My mate magic was gone but the love was still there. So were the longing and the need and the deep, core-knotting terror that this might truly be the end.

All those edge things one would expect when one dances on the surface of a bubble.

I must have blinked. Or maybe the shifting between elven order and fae chaos hit me again. Because I didn't remember stepping between Titania's charging stallion and the woman I loved.

I lowered my shoulder and held Sal out in front of me like a bar. If I got under the stallion's neck and low enough on his chest, I might be able to flip him. Sal pushed out a tilted shield spell very much like the one Arne had used earlier. She was not backing away from this fight. We had this.

The air directly above the fence line shimmered. Bloodyhoof manifested mid-jump, as if the fence was his own portal edge, Hrokr on his back and all his energy focused on the charging fae stallion.

Bloodyhoof rounded on his front legs, sidestepping and swinging around his hindquarters, and slammed side-to-side into Titania's stallion hard enough that a concussive wave of magic so bright I cringed hit me full in the face.

Troubles. Loneliness. The weight of expectations and the found momentary freedom of tricking one's way out of one's bonds. Then the wave was gone.

I sucked in my breath. Was that Hrokr? Loki? Titania? I had no idea. I blinked away the flash.

The ghost stallion vanished.

Bloodyhoof stood over me. Hrokr leaned down, his hand extended to help me onto the stallion, but he spoke to Ellie. "Let's go!"

I looked over my shoulder. She blinked, also stunned by the flare of magic. She wasn't more than ten paces farther down the fence line. Maybe eight. But she was too far away for me to reach her quickly.

Hrokr hadn't thought things through once again. He hadn't taken into account that Titania had already proven her portal magic still operated here. That she could move around at will, and easier than the elves.

The Queen's stallion manifested, once again, in mid-jump over the fence. His front legs hit the muddy ground directly behind Ellie and he stepped forward, his hindquarters coming down, and twisted ever so slightly so that his rider could reach down.

Titania grabbed the straps of Ellie's backpack and hauled her onto the stallion's back.

CHAPTER 17

The only way for me to vault onto Bloodyhoof was to hand Sal to a Loki elf.

Horkr hadn't called up a saddle or armor. I needed to vault onto the back of a draft-horse-sized enchanted stallion while carrying an extremely sharp weapon whose magic kept everyone but the elves and me from touching her.

Titania threw her daughter over the front of her stallion's newly-manifested saddle and bolted for the open field.

I looked up at Hrokr.

He didn't have any more of a poker face than I did. He knew exactly why I paused. And any hope we had of him shrugging off his anger and reactivity vanished.

"I can't touch the horse!" Sal said.

Arne, now on the fully-rigged white Percheron Comet, pointed at Titania as she rode by. "Go!" he yelled.

Magnus, on Lucky, galloped after the Queen.

I dropped Salvation onto the ground. "Sorry!" I said, and vaulted onto Bloodyhoof's back behind Hrokr.

Anger burst off Salvation. How many times was I going to leave her behind? There was an elf right there on the horse.

"Go!" I slapped Hrokr's shoulder. "I couldn't chance your enchantments interacting with the magic on her handle," I said.

It was an excuse. Hrokr knew it was an excuse, but he seemed to accept it, at least for the moment.

He slapped Bloodyhoof's neck. "Catch the kelpie, boy!"

Behind us, Arne magicked Sal off the ground and stowed her in his scabbard. Ahead, Magnus chased Titania and Ellie.

And the *kelpie*. "She brought through kelpies?" We couldn't let it through back into Alfheim. What if it took up residence in one of our lakes? Kelpies murdered mundanes every chance they got.

They murdered witches, too.

"I bet he's a handsome young man when he's in human form," Hrokr said. "Quite handsome, actually. More handsome than you."

Nothing about my reaction contained a thought-out response. Not for one splinter of a second did I think about the ramifications of my action, or the likely consequences, or the very real, bordering-on-visible reverberations it would cause into the future.

I planted my hand against Hrokr's shoulder and pushed.

He squeaked, obviously surprised, and tumbled off Bloodyhoof's side. "Hey!" he yelled.

We rode away, Bloodyhoof the magnificent stallion, and me, the man who'd just left Hrokr muddy and vulnerable.

The kelpie outpaced Lucky, and Magnus was falling behind even with a magic power boost to the Percheron's speed and stamina.

Horses as large and heavy as Bloodyhoof tire easily, but not Magnus's elven breeds. Bloodyhoof was as fast as a racehorse. I slapped the horse's neck. "Get the kelpie, boy," I said. "Show the fae who's best."

We overtook Magnus. He tossed me a confused look as if to ask why I chased a clearly dangerous fae. "Titania has the seer," I called.

The concealments had kicked in again, but Magnus understood *seer*. "She's hit the boundary," he said.

Magnus whipped a bright blue bolt of magic at Titania—no, not at the Queen. He whipped it in front of her, at the fence line.

Titania, on the greenish kelpie, jumped the pasture's far fence and directly into the bolt. The air wobbled and shimmered, and for a second I thought she'd taken Ellie through another portal, but they landed squarely on the service road on the other side.

All boundaries seemed to carry extra magic in the veil, which meant that at any time, any jump, any edge cut or ditch crossed, could be what Titania needed to vanish into her realm. Magnus's bolt must have diminished that magic, the same way Hrokr's had disrupted the routing magic in the first place.

We bolted for the fence.

"Frank! Don't—"

We jumped and…

We were still in the veil. Still on the surface of the bubble. Still on the service road but Magnus's farm and the pasture were farther away.

We were not in the same place.

I looked back. No Magnus. No Arne or Hrokr. No sheep or any living things other than Bloodyhoof, the kelpie, Titania, and Ellie.

The Dread Queen of the Fae reined the kelpie around. "Did you think an elf's magic would stop me, son?" she called.

Bloodyhoof snorted and sidestepped as if he wanted to ram the kelpie. I almost let him. We were alone with Titania. Alone in a place where we'd been cut off from all support—Norse elf and Celtic fae.

Yet we weren't. There were more pantheons out there. Gods of the mundanes who had heard Axlam's calls. I'd felt them in St. Martin's church.

"Why does this place look like Magnus's field?" I asked.

Titania cocked her head and looked at me from under her helmet's edge. "He's smarter than he looks, isn't he?" she asked.

"If you hurt him, I swear to you right now, Mother, you will *pay*," Ellie shouted.

More likely Titania would make her daughter pay.

"The cottage…" Ellie said.

"Let her go." Let the cottage do what it was meant to do. Let me find her once again.

Titania reined the kelpie around again. "This place looks like the handsome elf's world because the Loki elf's interference caused it to default to mimicking the exit point." The kelpie tossed his head but she expertly controlled his tantrum. "Otherwise it would have looked like where we were going."

What was more frightening here, the level of fae magic she'd just explained, or that she'd explained it to me? Now she could say I knew a secret.

I'm an idiot.

The cottage had wanted me to know that there was more magic under the heavens and on the earth than were dreamt of by fae. Magic Titania had harnessed to help build the cottage. The magic of the land. Of the stag and the eagle. Of cat and wolf and tree. World magic.

I slapped my hand over the Yggdrasil tattoo on the side of my face. "Please help," I said.

What was I doing? What was I calling?

Part of me suspected I'd just signed a deal far worse than anything the fae could offer. Or maybe not. Maybe this was part of the deal I'd already made with the cottage.

Ellie pounded her fists into her mother's armored leg. "Let me go, Mom! The—"

She stopped talking. She wrapped the fingers of one hand around the one thing every story said was the only means by which to make a kelpie pliable. The one magical item that kept them under control.

She wrapped her other arm up and around her back, and pressed down on her backpack as if making sure the bag was as much in contact with her body as possible.

Then she looked up at me. "I love you, Frank," she said.

Ellie vanished.

The cottage took her and all she held, including the kelpie's bridle.

CHAPTER 18

The cottage had taken Ellie. She was safe. I had to believe she was safe. I *would* believe she was safe. Not believing in her safety felt like a bullet hole from which I would bleed out in both body and mind.

If I still had my mate magic, I'd know. I'd feel if she was safe. I'd *know*.

But I wasn't sure. I couldn't be sure until I reached the cottage.

Or I got my mojo back.

I stared down at Titania. "Give me back what you stole," I growled.

She adjusted her antlered helmet and made a small motion toward the kelpie's head as if to tell me to shut my damned mouth in front of the evil fae.

I knew some of the stories about kelpies. About how they embodied the malevolence of dangerous waters, both as untamable horses and as handsome strangers who dragged their victims to their deaths.

The question was just how angry the kelpie Titania had bridled was, and whether or not he feared his Queen more than he wanted to give himself over to his rage.

This place favored the rage.

The kelpie's eyes turned bright, demonic red. He wail-whinnied a shriek so piercing and evil I cringed.

Titania should have just held onto his back and let him shriek. Violent acting out took a lot of fast twitch energy and he would have calmed down enough for her get control pretty quickly. But she didn't.

She slapped one of her gags onto the kelpie's muzzle.

The kelpie bucked and kicked. Titania was now on the back of a wild raging Scottish bronco and for a second, I felt sorry for her.

Only for a second.

The kelpie bucked her off. She twisted in the air like a cat and landed in a crouch too close to his lashing hooves. One of the kelpie's front legs hit one of the sharp, crystalline antlers.

Kelpie blood splattered across her front.

This time, the shriek moved *toward* the kelpie as if he pulled it back from the magic of the veil. It hit my back like a gale-force wind and grated against my ears like a sandstorm. The sound pushed on the kelpie, shrinking him down, and concentrating his magic into a smaller body.

A beautiful young man appeared, one strong and healthy with a head of large black curls. Blood dripped from under the edge of the black t-shirt covering his left bicep but he didn't seem to notice. He also wore a black modern-looking tactical kilt and big heavy boots, all with a strong paramilitary feel.

He picked up a rock and whipped it at Titania's head. Rapid, angry Gaelic followed. Then he turned toward me.

His eyes were the same green death color he'd been in horse form. "Oh, look. Another paladin," he said. "How special for ye."

I was no more a paladin than I was a jotunn. "I am not your enemy," I said.

He grinned. "I smell a lake on ye." He sniffed the air. "Smelled the same lake on th' magic the Queen kidnapped." He leaned forward. "No concealments can hide a healthy young thief from *me*."

Ellie's concealments worked on him, but not as well as they did other magicals. The cottage got her away, but she'd also taken his bridle.

I wanted Bloodyhoof to trample this miscreant into the magical soil of the veil, but I had a feeling that's what he wanted.

He wanted my horse, and I think my stallion knew it, too.

Bloodyhoof reared and met the kelpie's words with his own loud and strong *neigh*.

The kelpie laughed. "Aren't ye gonnae make a dash for it?"

Titania righted her helmet. "Dash for what?"

Oh, she knew he meant a dash for the cottage and my lake. I could tell from the extra flair in how she dusted her knees and the exaggerated wiggle of her torso. She was being contrary while showing dominance. She'd gone into full trickster stance.

The kelpie touched the gash on his arm, then rubbed his cheek and his lips, smearing blood across his face. "I *smell* her, mah Queen."

Titania stopped prancing. She looked up at me. "I don't know how you convinced the cottage to pull her back after I told it to *listen*, Frank Victorsson."

It *had* worked.

She held out her hands and her crystalline armor collapsed onto her body. "It's tired." The armor darkened into shimmering night-filled glass. "Which means it won't do what it needs to do until it has enough power."

It was still in Alfheim. It had called back its battery—but it needed to recharge. I had time. I could get to Ellie the way I had last night. I could find my way before the cottage closed up for the night, drained away Ellie's power, and moved her somewhere else.

The kelpie might get to her, too.

Titania pointed at the kelpie. "Tell Odinsson what he's dealing with now."

She vanished just as a new blast of magic hit my back.

The kelpie's eyes widened in terror and he turned to run into the corn field across the service road.

Arne jumped through first. Magnus appeared with Sal and her

scabbard in his hand. They reined the horses around as they watched the kelpie run between the harvested corn stalks.

Arne's All-Father surfaced, then sank back under his armor, then surfaced again in an oscillating brilliance I had no choice but to turn away from. Magnus's beauty, though, showed up the kelpie's handsomeness for what it really was: a mask.

Hrokr wasn't with them.

"Where is my son, Frank." Arne did not ask. He stated as if the loss of our Loki elf was my fault and that it was now my job to go find him.

"I have no idea where your boy is, Arne Odinsson." Yes, I'd pushed him off Bloodyhoof, but I was not a magical. Finding him in the shifting world of the veil would not be up to me. Nor was I going to apologize.

I had more important needs at the moment.

Magnus's eyebrow arched as if he was equally surprised and annoyed. He handed me Sal and the scabbard. "She led us to you," he said.

He's mine, rolled from the axe. Magnus chuckled. "You've been chosen, my good man."

I strapped Sal to my back. "We've already had this conversation, Salvation."

The throbbing possessiveness ceased as if she'd shut a window. It was still there, I was sure of it, but at least now she had the manners to keep it to herself.

I reined Bloodyhoof toward Arne. "Send me home." I looked toward Magnus. "I'll need a truck."

"No." Arne watched the kelpie run away. "We will have a war if Hrokr falls—"

"He's a Loki elf!" I yelled. The rage that this place whipped up suddenly manifested behind my eyes, and magic drifting behind the running kelpie shifted from his pale green to sickly orange. "He's your problem, not mine!"

"Frank..." Magnus said.

I pointed. "*He* smells my lake." He wanted only one thing—his bridle. How long before he transitioned into the part of the real world where he could get it? *"He* will do harm to…" Damn it. "To the seer if he gets away." I reined Bloodyhoof around again. "So *you* send me home *right now.*"

"Not without my son."

If he'd been on Bloodyhoof with me, I would have pushed him off, too. Intellectually, I knew finding Hrokr was a priority. I knew anger with the elves wouldn't get me what I needed. It didn't matter.

I slapped Bloodyhoof's rump. "Follow the kelpie, boy!" The kelpie wanted his bridle. He'd lead me where I needed to go.

Bloodyhoof didn't move. He tossed his head and looked to Magnus for instructions.

Magnus narrowed his eyes at Arne, but he spoke to me. "You had mate magic earlier, at the barn. I sensed it."

"Yes," I said. I'd hold my cool. I had no choice.

"It's gone."

"Titania stole it."

Magnus looked right at me. He sniffed. "You will need to deal with the kelpie on your own."

"I have Sal," I said.

My axe winked into alertness.

"Magnus Freyrsson…" Arne said.

They were not telling me everything, and honestly, I didn't care. "The kelpie's almost out of sight," I said.

Magnus stared defiantly at his king as he took a long, deep breath. Then he slapped the Yggdrasil tattoo on the side of my head. I didn't understand the incantation, but I felt it creep across my face.

He'd hit me with another muzzle. I yanked on Bloodyhoof's mane to turn him away. No more of this. I could still catch the kelpie even if—

A saddle manifested under me, and a bridle and reins on Bloody-hoof's head.

The spell Magnus had slapped onto my face fully wove itself over my face, but not over my mouth. It covered my eyes.

I saw all the magic. *All* of it. All the edges and the ebbs and the flows. I saw gates and pathways. Magnus had given me a way to see the natural routing magic of this place. I could find my own way home, if I had to.

The same spell manifested over Bloodyhoof's eyes, too.

Magnus swung Lucky around and slapped his hand across Sal's scabbard. "Do what you must to deal with what cannot be, Salvation." Then he pulled Lucky back and placed his hand on Bloodyhoof's neck. "Do what you must to get him where he needs to be, Blodughofi."

Then Magnus Freyrsson, Alfheim's elf of prosperity and fertility, slapped Bloodyhoof's rump.

The stallion knew what to do. We both knew what to do.

Together, we chased down a kelpie.

CHAPTER 19

The kelpie stayed twenty paces ahead. He wove. We dashed. He ducked. We lunged. Yet there he was, in the field, or along the stream, or under the trees, still twenty paces ahead. Every weave, or duck, or skid under logs allowed him to vanish from our view. He hid each time, attempting to use the magic of this place to out-maneuver Bloodyhoof, but Magnus had given us the elven equivalent of magical infrared night-vision goggles. The kelpie tried, but we compensated. Every rock jumped or railroad track crossed, we followed.

His goal was his bridle. My goal was getting to the cottage before it moved. Same place. Same Ellie. He would hurt her if he got there first.

And if he hurt her, I'd hurt him.

The kelpie would discover the level of damage my semi-dead body was capable of inflicting if he got to Ellie first.

The rage told me to kill him. To be the judge of his evil kelpie ways and twist his head from his body like I was pulling a cork from a bottle. Magical or not, that level of violence was also freeze-dried into my bones.

All the tales my father had told to that ship captain came with a grain of truth. I was capable of all the terror of which he accused me.

But I would not be the creature he created. I would not embody *his* fears.

I wouldn't embody the murderous glee of Victor Frankenstein.

Salvation wanted me to know that no matter what happened, she would always love me.

"You aren't helping," I said.

Yes, she was. I worried too much.

She was correct; I did worry too much. But what she worried about and what I worried about were not the same things.

Bloodyhoof galloped along, reacting to every slight shift in the magic around the kelpie, the ones that meant he used his magic to push his weaving and his ducking to their magical extremes.

I still knew deep down what was likely to happen when we crossed the boundary that took us back into the real world.

I had to catch him first.

We chased him through an open field, hopping row after row of harvested hay and chasing him around the big round bales. He vanished behind a bale.

Salvation and Bloodyhoof somehow compensated—the visible magic around us shifted—and the kelpie reappeared farther up, out from behind another bale.

The field also changed every time the magic shifted. We moved from the fields near Magnus's farm to land that reminded me more of the fields that butted up against Alfheim proper. Same drop. Same bales of hay. Yet we were getting closer and closer to the lake and the cottage.

Close enough that we'd hit the fence at the edge of the property in no less than ten gallops.

The kelpie looked over his shoulder. He threw me a rude Scottish gesture. And he ran directly into the fence.

It exploded.

Inward first, then as a peeling back outward roll of wood and nails and snow. It exploded and ceased, or opened, and I knew exactly what was on the other side.

CHAPTER 20

Bloodyhoof did not pause. His gait did not falter. Salvation gave him a burst of brilliant horse confidence and he leaped through the hole with me on his back.

His front legs came down on the gravel behind the glass and chrome monstrosity that was the Carlsons' house. We immediately skidded on the rocks, slowing as fast as the stallion could, so we didn't smack full into the building's side.

We were across the lake from my cabin, on the gravel drive that looped around my lawyer neighbor's too-expensive vacation home.

Magnus's magic-sensing enhancement had stayed in the veil. We were back to real world navigating by horse sense and my normal ability to see magic.

It'd have to do.

Aaron Carlson stood next to his BMW, a suitcase by his side and his mouth agape. His wife stood in the door of the house, face white as a sheet as if she was about to throw up.

They must have come up from The Cities for a long weekend and were unpacking their car.

Aaron pointed at the lake. "A man in a kilt hopped the fence and dove into the water." He, thankfully, knew about the magicals of Alfheim.

I reined Bloodyhoof around. We were on the opposite side of the lake from the cottage's peninsula.

The kelpie had a straight shot through the water. We did not.

"Aaron!" I said. "Call Bjorn Thorsson at Raven's Gaze. Tell him I'm chasing a kelpie." I reined Bloodyhoof toward the road. It'd be faster than going along the shore.

"Kelpie? Damn." He pulled his phone out of his pocket. "Claire! You and the girls stay away from the shore." He waved me off. "Go."

Sal wanted me to know that she liked this mundane man, though she could do without his terrified wife. Terrified wives were not warriors.

"Please stop," I muttered to my axe. "*Ha!*" I called and took Bloody-hoof up the driveway to the road. Thankfully the plows had come through, and the stallion quickly returned to a gallop.

I had no idea if we'd get there in time, or if the cottage had a way to ward off the kelpie. But we had to try.

We made the peninsula quickly and Bloodyhoof slowed to thread his way between the trees. We passed the red oak where the dryads had first appeared, then the leaning cedar. Each showed their normal level of natural magic. No signs of extra fae-borne contamination.

We broke through the trees into the space in front of the small fence surrounding Ellie's cottage.

Her home was still here. Still solid with no telltale extra magical energy signaling that it was about to move. We'd made it in time.

So had the kelpie.

He sat on the fence next to the gate, legs spread wide and knocking the heels of his boots against the fence post with a rhythmic *thump thump*.

He sniffed. "There ye are," he said in his otherwise lovely Scottish accent. "Here I thought I'd have to do this all by mah lonesome."

He held out his hand to call Bloodyhoof. The stallion ignored him.

We should kill him now, Sal pushed into my head. Kelpies were a level of danger that could not be left unchecked.

The kelpie frowned. "Gie off th' horse, ye ugly doughnut of a monster. Face me like a man."

Riding Bloodyhoof gave me an advantage. "Leave before I snap your neck," I said.

He laughed. "Oh, ye pathetic animated pile o' corpse dung." He slapped his chest. "She's gonnae give me mah bridle, d'ye understand? She stole mah property, an' she's gonnae *pay*." His face cinched up and he sniffed at the air. "I smell it clear as day, her protection enchantments be damned."

Was he following the bridle or Ellie? I couldn't parse how much of what he said was bluster from how well he could sense Ellie through the concealments.

"They *all* pay, the lasses," he said. "Dumb little fillies, aye? Come too close, they do, and th' loch, it calls me." He slapped his chest again. "Someone's got tae teach th' lessons."

I could offer to broker the bridle in exchange for him leaving, but I didn't think he'd go without inflicting some evil. They *all* pay, after all. If it wasn't Ellie, it'd be Aaron's wife and daughters. Or Akeyla. Or Sophia. He'd find at least one lass to harm before he made his way back to his homeland.

One cannot reason with a kelpie, Sal pushed.

"Oh, look at ye! Big mean paladin. Thinkin' about how to save th' world, are ye? Good on ye." He slapped his knee. "Is that lady of an axe talkin' to ye?" He slapped his knee again. "O' course she is." He shook his head.

"Every elf in Alfheim knew the moment you touched one of their lakes," I said.

He threw his arms wide. "An' yet not one of your wankpuffin mates has come to help ye or your *lovely* lass, my dear walkin' mound o' goblin excrement." He closed one eye and pretended to peer at me as if reading the world from my expression. "I wonder how come that is."

He understood Ellie's concealments.

The bridle is part of him, Sal said.

So part of him had, like me, gotten inside the enchantments. And now that part was no longer affected. But from the way he sniffed the air, his breaking of the concealments was only partial—or the cottage was actively fighting him.

Kill him, Sal said.

I knew Sal was correct—the danger this kelpie presented ranged well beyond the threat to the town St. Martin had carried in with him. It ranged beyond his clear and present danger to Ellie. She had me. She had the cottage.

If the kelpie got away, he'd go on a murder spree. "If I chop off your legs, you won't be able to run to the lake," I said.

He frowned. "She's gonnae give herself tae me willingly. They always do, y' brutish plum."

A flare of magic moved along the far roofline of the cottage's new sunroom addition. Someone with exceptionally high amounts of natural magic was creeping along back there, doing her best to keep quiet and invisible.

Ellie. She'd come out the door on the other side of the cottage and was sneaking up on the kelpie, who sensed her but couldn't see her.

I would not look and give away her presence. The magic roaring up and over the roof rivaled the intensity of anything I'd seen from the elves and I had no idea what that meant, or how she would use it, or if she could, or…

Or if she'd get hurt.

And for the second time in all this, the hole left behind by my stolen mate magic became a gulf. We weren't connected and I had no idea, or feeling, or gut understanding, data, words—anything—to tell me a truth I could trust. I was out here as blind as the kelpie and full of every single yearning and need and desire I'd experienced this morning but without the safety net.

No matter what I did, the certainty that the woman I loved wasn't going to reject me had evaporated at Titania's hands.

And there it was, the most familiar and agonizing of all the knives in my gut.

The kelpie peered at me. "Och, ye poor dear laddie." He leaned toward Bloodyhoof. "Ye *yearn*." He clapped his hands. Bloodyhoof *neighed* and tossed his head, but reading my emotions held the kelpie's attention.

Ellie rounded the corner of the addition, her back against the wall and a baseball bat in her hand. Her magic coiled in opposite directions from itself as green, blue, and a scattering of red flame-like licks. She moved as a double helix of power.

I'd never, not once in all her time in Alfheim, seen anything other than mundane-level wisps of magic around her body. The cottage always drained it off at night.

It wasn't drained right now.

The kelpie hopped off the fence. "Will she love ye when this is all said an' done? I doubt it." He sniffed the air, leaned back against the rail, and smirked up at me. "She knows what ye are. She loves the idea o' an attack dog." He sniffed the air again. "Until that dog kills somethin' in front o' her. Lasses dinnae like guts on the floor."

Killing him might make everything he'd just said come true. Ellie might turn away. I put my hand on Sal's handle anyway.

"That's how ye show all yer ugliness, paladin. All those scars take on meanin' when ye slice an' dice, aye?" He sniffed once more and his face crunched up as if he was confused about something.

Ellie ran across the yard, bat up and aimed at his head.

I needed to keep his attention. Once Ellie smacked him and he was down, I'd get between them. "Shut up, kelpie!" I barked.

He glared and pointed up at me. "*I* ne'er kill where th' lasses can see! I'm th' beauty that lets them—"

The bat slammed against his right temple with enough force to knock him sideways. He rolled with it, twisting around and doing a header over the fence into the yard.

I slapped Bloodyhoof's neck. "Jump the fence, boy!"

Ellie swung the bat again. "Submit, kelpie!" she screamed.

Bloodyhoof backed up to do as asked, but stopped.

The kelpie roared as he stood up. "Submit tae what, lass?" He rolled his shoulders. "I smelled ye but I couldn't see ye beyond th' fence. Nice of ye tae knock me in from th' other side." He rubbed the side of head. "Where's mah bridle, mah sweet an' lovely mistress?"

"Bloodyhoof..." I said. He wouldn't jump the fence.

"I burned it," Ellie said.

The kelpie laughed. "Ye did no such thing, sweets. I'd *know.*"

The place of the helpful fae magic is beyond the fence, isn't it? Sal asked.

"Yes," I said.

The stallion is like the kelpie. He's seeing one thing and smelling another. That's why he won't jump.

"You can't hurt me." Ellie held the bat between them. "The rules say that whoever has the bridle controls the kelpie."

The kelpie laughed again. "Let's talk about what *control* means, shall we?" He quickly thrust his chest out to scare and startle Ellie.

"You gotta trust me," I said to the horse. "You'll be safe if you take the leap."

Ellie's magic condensed down toward her, but it didn't respond as if she could direct it toward the kelpie. "Let the elf horse in!" she yelled.

The energy around the cottage shifted and the boundary at the fence pushed toward us as if reaching out to Bloodyhoof. The horse snorted.

Salvation pushed out her own inquiry to the cottage's magic.

The horse can enter, Sal said. *I cannot. I am dangerous.*

So was I.

The kelpie slapped his chest again. "Ye need tae be specific, lass," he drawled.

He was too close to Ellie. She held her ground, but the kelpie was taller and stronger.

I could drop Sal again. I could leave her behind. But I'd promised not to allow the fae to get her, and if the kelpie jumped the fence again, she'd be vulnerable. I was pretty sure I'd allowed the fae to get Hrokr. And that kelpie—

"Let Salvation through!" I yelled at the cottage. At the world. At the giant ash tree in the yard and at the kelpie. "Please," I whispered.

The air shifted toward warmth as if the world had stepped back from its winter dormancy and decided to hold onto its summer life.

Bloodyhoof tossed his head. His front quarters tensed, then his hind. And the three of us jumped the fence into the cottage's yard.

I don't know if the cottage listened to me, or if something else did, but my horse rammed the kelpie into the ash tree with such force I heard bones snap.

I jumped off the horse.

The kelpie panted and thrust his chin at Ellie. "I'm gonnae drag ye under an' eat yer eyeballs, ye pissy little frog-faced—" he yelled.

I curled my hand around his throat. "My axe wants to cut you in half." I pulled Sal from her scabbard and swung her blade at the tree just above his head. I stopped her momentum a fraction of an inch before cutting into the bark. I did, though, skim curls off his head.

He yelped when Ellie pressed the end of the bat into his wounded shoulder. "You can't intimidate us when we're both on the same side of the fence, now can you?"

He groaned. I grinned.

"*Control* means you do as commanded," Ellie said. "Do you understand that you must submit to and follow the commands of the individual who possesses your bridle?"

"Yes," the kelpie hissed.

"I command you to go back to your loch," Ellie said. "I command you to inflict no more harm. You are to say nothing of me or my home. You will listen for my call, and when I desire your company, you will come. Do you understand these commands?"

The kelpie groaned. "Yes," he hissed out like a deflating tire.

"If you break these commands, I will destroy you and your bridle. Do you understand the consequences?"

"Yes," he hissed out a third time.

She pointed the gate. "Leave."

We need to kill him, Sal said.

The helix of magic around Ellie flared up toward the sky. "Not yet," she responded.

The kelpie looked confused.

Ellie snarled. Her eyes shimmered dark with the cosmos. Magic flared from their sides in much the same way as it had from Hrokr's while we were in the veil—like a witch about to overheat. "I will string a violin with your entrails, horse." Her voice echoed between the cottage and the trees. "I will drain your loch and burn your bones."

He blinked. "Witch," he breathed.

"Kelpie in five pieces," she responded as she moved her hand to indicate the chopping off of his head and limbs.

He blinked rapidly as he worked his face away from his terror and into a mask of pure, unadulterated hate. He pointed at me. "Ye're gonnae pay, dead boy."

Magical dust blossomed around Ellie as if her emotions had exploded into a sweet, lovely firework. It burst up and out, then flowed down her shoulders, over her arms, to settle around her hands.

"Harm my mate and I will geld you with a dull saw blade, you pathetic excuse for a fae," Ellie said.

She will, Sal said.

I had no doubt that if we didn't drain off her overheating magical power, she would—and that she might not be able to stop with just the kelpie.

"Listen to Titania's daughter," I growled.

The kelpie slowly pushed off the tree and limped toward the gate. He stopped just before crossing and looked over his shoulder. His lips thinned to a line.

He stepped through and disappeared, hopefully forever.

CHAPTER 21

Most of the snow had melted. Dripping icicles hung from the roofline over the cottage's big window, each glistening in the early evening sun. The remainder of a drift leaned against the cottage, and every time melt water landed in the crispy snow, it crackled and cracked like an iceberg.

Bloodyhoof pawed at the mud and nibbled on the little bit of grass still available. Up in the tree, a jay called. Somewhere out in the woods, a raven answered. The cottage's ash rustled in the slow, cold breeze. And Ellie shimmered like a goddess of chaos.

She stared at the gate as if waiting for the kelpie to crawl back on his hands and knees begging her to rip him to pieces.

"Ellie," I said.

She twitched and continued to stare at the gate. "Kelpie's blood burns *bright*," she muttered.

A century ago I watched the same thing happen to Rose. The same fires. The same mutterings about blood and magic. The elves helped then. They couldn't now.

"Hey. Hey, honey. Look at me." I touched her shoulder.

Her overheating witch power ripped up my arm and into my

shoulder socket, and I pulled back my hand as if I'd just touched a hot stove.

Dark power pulsed out the sides of her eyes. She looked at my hand, blinked twice, and her face contorted into the same mask of pain and self-hate I'd seen on Hrokr.

Her body resisted her natural fae power and it was eating her alive.

Fire blipped through my mind, not as a word or a memory or anything that made conscious sense. *Fire* surfaced uncalled and unwanted from the feral depths as tunnel vision and a pounding heart.

But the part of my mind that sits just under the part that over-thinks the world knew this particular flashback all too well, and took its own immediate action—I jerked back not from Ellie, but from myself.

She didn't notice. She stared at her own hand as if she also could see the power swirling around her body. "The cottage is confused." She blinked again. "It made a decision. It minimized part of the concealments to let in the horse and the axe. It's never made a decision before."

Hello?... Calm down.... Sal called.

She wasn't talking to me.

Ellie's brow furrowed.

In my head, Sal's voice stammered. *He's mine!*

Ellie lifted her face to the sky. "No, Salvation," she snapped.

Sal didn't answer. Her attention wasn't on us.

"She's talking to the cottage." I put my axe back in her scabbard. "Honey, you're burning up." *Fire* flitted through my mind again. *Keep it together*, I thought. "Did you block the cottage from draining away your power?" Without her power, the cottage couldn't move. But holding back that power was killing her.

She was breathing too fast. "Mom told the cottage to take me home. She *touched* it and she *told* it to take me to her realm if I got away from her because she does that. She's a trickster. She's terrible and she can make anyone and anything do whatever she wants!" She stomped her foot. "The cottage doesn't have a choice. It has to play out the spell, but it doesn't want to. It wants to stay here. We landed in this land, and it touched you, and suddenly it's *thinking*. It's *alive*. It's afraid that if we leave, it'll lose its new awareness. It needs you, Frank, as much as it needs me. So it stopped siphoning." She looked down at her hands. "It's only been a few minutes. I... I hid the bridle and the cottage asked what to do and we *agreed*."

I pulled her against my chest. Her power screamed through me like I'd just hooked jumper cables to my hands and it took significant concentration not to twitch or yell or push away.

Flames blipped through my mind again, along with another flash of an even deeper trauma—a cold slab, blinding lightning, thunder as pulsing as the electricity through my dead nerves.

My mind knew this particular flashback. It also knew what it was about to dredge up.

"I'm here," I said, through the haze of glare reflecting off my own charged-up, dithering, foaming life of rejection. Off the byproducts of the scars and the scariness, and the ugly and the lumbering. Every bit of the fear generated by the sucking away of my mate magic.

Understanding my traumas didn't stop them from surfacing. All it ever did was give me words to describe the episodes after the fact.

A sob burst from deep in Ellie's chest. "Frank!"

"If the cottage restarts its siphoning, it'll move, won't it?" I asked.

"Yes," she said into my chest. "I want to burn things," she whispered.

My axe had been talking to the cottage. "Salvation! A little help here, please."

She wanted us to know that the cottage had a thick accent and they weren't communicating well but they were trying.

I pressed my cheek against Ellie's head and a new electrical jolt spread a thick coat of metallic-tasting buzz across my tongue. I fought back the need to spit. "It'll be okay," I said.

"No, it won't." She buried her face in my neck. "We wanted to stay. We wanted to say good-bye." She hiccupped. "I thought... I thought if you knew for sure that she'd taken us to her realm the elves might be able to help you find me."

"You're not going anywhere." She was not going back to Titania's realm. Not alone. I hoisted her up and curled her legs around my waist. The jolts increased in frequency and strength, but I held on anyway. "Can the cottage move Sal and me?" I wasn't going to lose Ellie, too.

You, perhaps, Salvation said. *Me, no. We don't have enough time to do the necessary magical translations.*

"Salvation, if I put you on Bloodyhoof, can you guide him to the cabin?" She'd be safe with the elves.

I will not be defeated, she yelled in my head.

"Sal..." My fears also radiated off my axe—the fear of rejection from the one I loved. The fear that I was not worthy of the life I had built in the community in which I'd built it. The fear that I wasn't nearly as alive as I thought I was. All the emotions my knotted flashbacks had tied up in their unwanted blips and bursts.

All those things that gave others reasons to reject a semi-dead thing.

Damn it, I thought.

Go, Blodughofi! Salvation yelled. *Go to Maura Dagsdottir.*

The stallion reared up. Then he galloped through the gate and into the trees beyond.

Frustration rode in on the back of my shocked and terrified nerves. Frustration with my own brain, with Sal's mirroring of my pain, with the very real possibility of losing Ellie because I wasn't smart enough to figure this out.

But also frustration because this punishment had descended onto Ellie because she'd tried to stay with me.

My mate magic might be gone, but we still had what we'd built despite the concealments keeping us apart. She trusted me. I needed to trust that I could trust her.

And all of a sudden, my body rolled up all the events of the past month and honed them into a sharp, terrible animosity toward all things royal and fae.

Was it misdirected? Yes. But it also cut through the buzzing, distracting haze in my brain. No one stole my faith.

Salvation yanked up my anger and added it to her own. *We will not be defeated*, she said again.

"We will not," I looked around. "There has to be some way to anchor the cottage." Nothing in the yard stood out. "Should we go inside?" Maybe something inside would let us anchor.

The magic swirling around Ellie brightened to near blinding. "I've tried to build an anchor. I tried in Tokyo and when it moved, it hurt Chihiro. She was inside with me. We can't go in."

"Okay. Okay," I said. We'd stay outside. "If only I still had my tracer spells, huh?" I said. I'd be able to find her easily no matter what her mother did.

Ellie hiccupped again. "I'm glad they're gone. Those damned things *hurt.*"

They interacted with her concealments. The vampires stole all of them anyway when they used me to...

Dracula used me as a siphon to concentrate his spells and stabilize Vampland.

I could do it again. I could drain off her extra energy.

"Salvation! Will it work?"

You will not, she said.

"You want to better Titania, don't you?" We both wanted to beat Titania at her own game. *We will not be defeated*, I thought at my axe. So it would work. It *had* to work. "What—"

"Blood magic," Ellie said.

You will not, Sal repeated. *I will not cause you harm.*

"Cut you. Drain you. Kill you." Ellie held tight to my neck and waist. "No no no no *no no no!*"

Blood magic is too dangerous.

We didn't have time to argue. Ellie's magic burned my eyes and set every hair on my body on end. She wasn't that far from burning out. "I'll be all right." I was always all right. "What's the point of being half-dead if I can't use it to our benefit?"

"You are *not* half-dead," Ellie said. "I know you had mate magic in the truck." She pulled her face away from my neck. "I know Mom stole it from you." She leaned her forehead against my chest. "Mine manifested the night after the elves got you out of Vampland."

She held up her hand and there, inside the torrent of her over-heating witch magic, spun bright blue mate magic dust.

All this time, the cottage must have been draining it off with all her other magic.

"You will not sacrifice yourself for us, Frank Victorsson," Ellie said. "Even if we are apart, I need to know you're okay." She inhaled sharply. "You *have* to be okay."

Now was not the time of death and sacrifice. I wouldn't allow it to be. I was done with the loss and the pain.

I kissed her deeply. "We're going to be okay."

A new sob broke free and she clung to me as I looked around the yard again.

Blood magic, I thought. Would a little blood on the cottage wall work? There had to be something other than Sal I could use to cut my arm. I looked back at the ash tree. Even a pointy stick might work.

"Your tattoo…" Ellie pulled away from my neck again.

"What?" Fire crept up my neck and into the spaces inside my Yggdrasil tattoo as if Ellie's magic was filling all the spaces the cottage emptied of St. Martin's magic.

"It's glowing," she said.

Blood magic transcended the elves and the fae. It touched the ancient beating heart of the planet, which was why it held so much power. Blood magic might be what I needed to siphon off enough of Ellie's magic to allow the cottage to stay in Alfheim.

I touched the side of my face. Then I turned, still holding Ellie, toward the ash tree.

I've sat at a bar with the World Raven. I've stood in a magic place— one not all that different from the elves' Great Hall—in the presence of a Wolf that was almost-but-not-quite the World Wolf. And I had the Norse version of the World Tree tattooed onto the side of my head.

The night I walked through the blizzard and into this very yard, I'd seen the stag under that tree's branches. I'd seen the squirrel, eagle, and hawk in her canopy. Deep down, I'd understood.

I'd understood later, too, in the dream.

There were other magicks here. Magicks older than elves and fae. Magicks that touched the seasons, night and day, life and death equally.

And yet I could not describe what I felt. It sat under words, in that feral place where I controlled nothing, and it swirled up into my consciousness only when it wanted to. Just like all the stress generated by the uncalled memories.

I lifted Salvation off my back.

Do not—

"Trust me, Salvation," I said.

I set Ellie down next to the ash's trunk. "I need both hands for this," I said, as I nicked the inner forearm of my dominant arm with Sal's blade before transferring her back into my hand.

"Frank. Don't." Fire trickled out the edges of her eyes. "Let me go." She gritted her teeth. "The cottage can't hold off any longer. If you hurt yourself—"

I kissed her again. "I love you," I said against her lips. Ellie needed to hear me say it. Honestly, I needed to hear myself say it. I should have told her earlier, but I had my rules. Insta-romance chaos wasn't going to break the steps I'd built to *me*—except *me* needed to be more than my ways of being.

She wrapped her arms around me and I hoisted her up against the trunk, leaning in and holding her in place with my hips.

"Unzip our jackets," I said.

She blinked.

"More contact."

She wiggled in her hand and pulled down first her zipper, then mine. Then she threaded her cold hands under my t-shirt and placed them in the middle of my back.

I was the warm one in all this, and I was about to get warmer.

"Forgive us," I said to the tree.

Ellie sucked in her breath. She closed her eyes.

I slammed Salvation's blade into the trunk of the ash.

CHAPTER 22

When I was in the Union Army, I took several bullets to the gut. If I'd been a mundane man, I would have died on the battlefield. The balls rattled around in my innards for a decade and a half afterward, pressing here and distorting there. Most of my life up until that point had been pressings here and distortions there, so a little lead made no difference. At that time of my life, nothing made much difference.

Dagrun, in an afternoon fit of motherly annoyance, unceremoniously magicked the lead out through a slit over my left hipbone. "There," she'd said. "Now heal yourself and stop complaining." Then she'd dropped seven bullets in a tin cup and walked away.

That was my first real lesson in how well my body acclimated to circumstance. I was stalwart. I stood against all gales. I bent. I didn't break no matter how much I fed my own wounds.

I used that acclimation to excuse a century's worth of whiskey. Dracula used it when he stuck a pike through my chest.

Time to put it to real use.

Sal's blade sliced in until her runes were buried in the tree's wood. I pressed my bleeding arm against the tree's bark as I held onto Salvation's handle. The purple magic that allowed me to hold her pulsed in rhythm with my heart, as did the tattoo. Next to Ellie's shoulder, I dug in the fingers of my other hand, and under her bottom, I pushed in a knee.

My roots grew deep into the well of my two-hundred-plus years. Some of what I drew up fouled the waters of my mind, but most of it didn't. The trick was to filter so only the best reached the leaves closest to the sun.

And my sun was about to be ripped from me because of the spells of her fae mother.

The ash tree understood. It also fought for clean roots and clear skies. It also stood stalwart and against all gales.

Blood to blood, it said, deep down in the World parts. *Breath to breath.*

Ellie screamed against my chest. The tree picked up every frequency in her voice and everything turned white—the bark, the magic coiling around us and into us, the snow, the sky, Salvation, the cottage. Everything became a ghost of itself as if the gain in the vision processing parts of my brain had been turned all the way up.

The buzz on my skin ramped up to a lightning strike. I gritted my teeth, and held on.

"I'm hurting you," Ellie said.

Buzz. Jolt. Blinding nothingness. Pain.

Breathe, said the tree, and...

The world was struggling with its own doubts and flashbacks, frustration and anger, death and destruction, but the World Tree did what it always did—it stood. It breathed. It grew and it became a forest. It took the worst, and if it burned up, it sprouted anew from its roots.

It did it for itself. It did it for its sun. It lived because living was its purpose.

The cottage pushed away Ellie's power instead of siphoning it into its enchantment engines. Sal called that power to her, and drew it up from my connection to Ellie.

Salvation released it into the tree.

Every branch shook. All remaining leaves fell to the muddy ground. The tree took every ounce of living, burning energy.

Behind us, the cottage implemented the commanded spell to move, but with empty batteries. The spell wove itself weakly around the building and the yard, dancing along the boundary of the fence, and in the whiteness overlaying my vision, I swore that for just a second I saw the too-blue sky of Titania's realm.

Then it was gone, vanished into the ghostly brilliance.

The cottage was the first to fall into unconsciousness. Salvation followed as the vast amount of power she channeled overwhelmed her mind. Between my chest and the tree, Ellie sucked in her breath as her connection to her cottage reset to its default siphoning.

All the remaining free power flowed from Ellie, to me, through Sal, and into the ash tree. The blinding whiteness diminished, and the golden early-evening light returned. The electrical agony vanished into a post-fire buzz. My muscles loosened.

The trees beyond the gate stayed the same. Jays called. My lake lapped against its shores and my cabin stayed just down the path.

Ellie dropped her legs to the ground but held tight to my waist. She was okay. I was okay. Sal and the cottage were okay, if drained.

The ground under my feet moved.

I tipped away from the tree, releasing my grip on Sal and carrying Ellie with me, and fell onto my backside.

Every branch and twig of the tree shimmered with real and magical light as if millions of fireflies had come to paint its branches with the evening's light.

"Oh, wow…" Ellie said.

I ran my hands up and down her back. "Are you okay? I felt the cottage start its siphoning again."

"Everything reset." She pointed at the tree. "Look."

The shimmer evaporated from the outer branches, then the next in, as the tree pulled Ellie's magic downward.

It was healing itself.

I scrambled to my feet and yanked Salvation from the bark just as the tree's shimmer increased to a real glow. The slice blazed for a moment, then closed as if Sal's blade had only nicked the bark.

The ground jerked. I stumbled and tripped, landing on the ground next to Ellie once more.

The remaining magic drained downward from the trunk and into the ground.

Ellie dropped her ear to the leaf litter. "I think the tree is rooting." My beautiful girlfriend smiled as she reached for me. "We're rooted to Alfheim."

I hugged her to my chest. Could it be true? Had the tree over-written part of Titania's complicated concealments?

Ellie yawned. I yawned. My mind wanted to mull and plan, but my brain would have none of it. *Breathe* filtered up. *Breathe* and *rest*.

But snow and mud did not make for a bed.

"We should go—" Yet I was asleep with my head on a pile of leaves and my arms around the woman I loved before I finished my sentence.

CHAPTER 23

S heep lips nibbled on my ear and I was suddenly completely
awake.

We'd fallen asleep out in the cold, in the mud, but I was dry, warm, and inside a pile of fresh, sweet-smelling hay heaped so high I couldn't really make out much of the world beyond the straw and the lamb's fluffy head.

The sheep sniffed at my face. His little nose wiggled, and he licked my cheek.

I knew this lamb. I'd carried him up to the barn while in the veil. "Do you mind?" I wiggled to get away from the next lick, but Ellie slept snuggled in under the hay and next to my side. She sighed and smacked her lips, and instead of rolling away, rolled against my hip. I didn't dare move.

The lamb laid a full lick onto my face from my jaw all the way to my hairline.

I swatted at him, trying to shoo him away. He backed up a bit but stopped when his butt hit another sheep.

Bells rang. *Baas* and *bleats* filled the air. I lifted my head as best I could to get a look around. We were still in Ellie's yard, inside the fence and under the ash tree. The cottage looked the same in terms of its size and layout. No extra overheating magic filled the air. Morning sun spread out over the roofline and set the remaining icicles glowing. And Sal slumbered in her scabbard nearby, close enough I could feel her presence, even if I couldn't see her at the moment.

Someone had lifted us out of the cold mud and put us into the warm heap of hay currently feeding not just the lamb, but at least thirty other sheep.

"Good morning, my sweet princeling."

I startled and rolled back toward Ellie.

Titania leaned over her daughter as she peered at my face. "Why, aren't you the problem solver!" She winked.

She'd changed out of the stolen dryad armor into a tightfitting white snow-bunny ski jacket and matching pants, complete with white gloves and a pair of goggles sitting on Ellie's bright yellow pompom hat.

"Titania," I said.

"You remember my name. Good. Do you remember your own, young man?" She nodded toward the tree as if to insinuate that it had drained a lot more than energy.

"Frank Victorsson," I said.

"And who's your daddy?" She grinned like a trickster.

"I am the adopted son of the King and Queen of Alfheim, Arne Odinsson and Dagrun Tyrsdottir."

She nodded sagely. "Good answer."

I snorted.

Titania bopped her daughter's nose. Ellie sighed again. Her fingers wiggled next to her face, but she didn't wake up.

"She does the sleeping princess thing *so well.*" Titania grinned. "Your little plan worked exactly as it was supposed to."

Why was I surprised the Queen of the Fae had known exactly what would happen? Then again, maybe she hadn't. Maybe she just wanted me to think she had. "I don't think the cottage will move again, even if you try to force it," I said.

She shrugged. "Not my problem anymore."

All the hell she'd caused, and she shrugged it off? "What about your husband?" I asked.

Titania stood up straight and pressed her fists into her waist in a very Akeyla-like move. "The handsome elf gave me half his sheep and several hives of his finest honeybees in exchange for... things."

I carefully pulled my arm out from under Ellie and sat up. "What things, Titania?" A deal had been struck, but with what consequences? There were always consequences.

She grinned and shrugged again.

But that grin vanished into her awe-invoking Dread Queen stare. "Neither your King, his Second, nor I wish to face the next Ragnarok unarmed." She looked up at the top of the ash tree. "I am afraid that such deals, while they ease the tension of the monarchs, make the lives of our paladins much, much more difficult."

The ease granted by the magical sleep evaporated into tightening neck and back muscles. Those consequences would come calling, and probably soon. "And what precisely do you mean by that, Queen Titania?"

She touched the tip of her nose, then pointed at me. "The thing is, my dear big ball of exhilarating handsomeness, that you're not *really* the Odin elves' paladin, now are you?" She nodded sagely once more.

I wasn't anyone's paladin. Except, perhaps, the woman sleeping next to me. I'd fight to the death to protect her.

The sweetness of the smile lighting up Titania's face surprised me, and when she leaned in and stroked my cheek, I was just as surprised by the tenderness of the touch. "What did my daughter call that expression? Your lack-of-poker face?" She kissed my lips. "I will bet on you any day, my dear young man."

I think my mother-in-law likes me, danced through my head as uncalled and random as any of my more problematic thoughts.

Titania pulled the goggles down around her neck and laid the hat gently next to Ellie's head. "I will give you a boon for your defense of my daughter."

Don't do it, I thought. Never ever make deals with the fae. Except this fae liked me. And I was already one hundred percent in. "… Okay," I said.

Her fingers danced. She shifted her feet, wound up her arm, and pitched a ball of magic at my face.

I took it head on. It'd hit me no matter what, so why not let the fae magic do what the fae magic was going to do?

It hit with a twinkle and a tingle, and burst into a bright cloud of magical dust.

She'd given me back my mate magic.

"Thank you," I said.

Titania looked out over her new flock of healthy, happy, prime New Zealand sheep. "Nice to see that Odinsson raised you with good manners," she said. "Kids these days don't know their pleases and thank-yous from a hole in their brain-sucking machines." She mimicked dancing her thumbs over a phone screen.

I chuckled.

The Queen of the Fae laughed. "You fought well for my daughter," she said. "You and that jealous axe of yours." She pointed at the ground next to our pile of hay.

Sal and her new scabbard rested on her own dry pile just out of reach.

The scabbard looked different. The bag was the same, but small tendrils of green and red magic danced with the blue and purple elven enchantments.

Titania touched her lips and shook her head as if to tell me not to speak of what I saw. I nodded to indicate that I understood.

"Ragnarok is a cycle." She stared out at the sky. "But I suspect you understand that already."

I didn't want to think about Ragnarok right now. I just wanted a day of touches with Ellie.

Titania looked me right in the eye, as if to say *listen*. "The new one's been in the making for two-hundred-plus years." And then the Queen of the Fae, and all her sheep, vanished.

Two-hundred-plus years. The length of time since my rebirth. And Brother's.

I looked down at Salvation. She'd been forged in the fires of a Ragnarok.

A small, weird little thought poked at the back of my mind: Had I been, as well?

Ellie stirred. She stretched and yawned, and wiggled like an exquisite cat. "Is this…" She picked up a handful of hay. "Straw?"

My mate magic welled up around my hands. It wanted to touch. *I* wanted to touch—but I was morning cold, even with the magical hay. "I think your mom wanted to make sure we didn't freeze during the night."

"My mom was here?" She looked around. "Did she do something terrible again?" A sniff followed. "I smell sheep."

I laughed. "Let's go in." It'd give me a chance to warm up. "I'll tell you everything over coffee."

"*Hmmm…*" She pouted. "But the hay smells so nice."

Ellie snuck her dusty fingers under my shirt and tickled my abs.

We had a lot to talk about, and a lot to figure out. Sal and the cottage both still slept. I needed to check in with the elves. We didn't know if her concealments had changed, or if Arne had found Hrokr, or…

Ellie pushed her hands down into the waist of my pants.

The overthinking stopped. I smiled.

We had a few hours. The world could wait.

EPILOGUE

I.

The shore of Frank's lake, Alfheim, Minnesota....

Hrokr Arnesson sat on a cold boulder on the edge of the lake's sloshing water. He clutched his book friend, the one with "Rygnyrök" scrolled across its leather cover in classic jotunn script, close to his chest.

The horrid Queen of the Fae stole his sheep friends, and her equally horrid daughter turned his not-a-jotunn friend away from him. His book friend wouldn't be going home to the fae-witch's library. Not now. Not ever. Not after Victorsson unceremoniously dumped him off the side of Blodughofi like a sack of whale bones. (Hrokr had *tried*. He'd tried *so hard*. One tiny little miniscule joke to relieve the tension and *bam*! That was it for poor Hrokr.)

Not to mention Arne's—Hrokr refused to call him "father" anymore—ice-cold stare and twitching lip when he'd kicked his son out of the veil and back into his "no bother" zone.

He'd been as angry about Hrokr *not* coming to him about the dryads as he was about Hrokr's "interference" with "his" seer, as if the witch's photographs were more important than his own son.

Arne Odinsson and Magnus Freyrsson had supplemented Hrokr's concealments right then and there because, like Victorsson, they had the most fragile of feelings.

He had options, though. Options that would not meet Arne Odinsson's and his oh-so-pretty Freyr elf sidekick's approval.

Hrokr rubbed at his nose and watched the woods. Lots was going on over at the cottage. Fae magic rolled through the trees like the fog from that horror story he'd read a couple of years ago—the one his vampire friend Tony Biterson had given him. Tony sure did know his pop culture.

"The Mist." That's what it was called. Some mundane with a royal name wrote it decades ago. There'd been nasty stuff in that haze, too.

Branches crashed. Saplings snapped. Titania's kelpie ran out of the trees spewing at least three languages' worth of swear words. He stopped at the shore, turned his back to the lake, and lifted his kilt in a grand show of Scottish crassness.

"Kelpie!" Hrokr shouted.

The kelpie dropped his kilt and sniffed at the air.

Arne's supplemental enchantments were more annoying than Victorsson's antics. But kelpies could smell a good yearning ten miles away, and Hrokr was only thirty feet down the shore, so there was hope.

Hrokr gazed longingly at the kelpie's perfectly proportioned—if bleeding—bicep. His low body fat percentage was the stuff of legends. Hrokr fanned himself and thought about how lovely it would be to run his fingers through the kelpie's lush ebony locks.

The kelpie sniffed again. His eyes narrowed and he turned in Hrokr's direction.

"Yesssss," Hrokr said. "Come to me, my *gor-gee-ousss* murder pony."

The kelpie sauntered along the shoreline, sniffing the air and careful of the bigger washed up logs, until he stood directly in front of Hrokr's boulder. "I smell an elf," he said, even as he didn't bother to look at the obvious in front of him.

Hrokr stood. He dusted his knees, tucked the book under his jacket, and extended his hand. "Prince Hrokr Lokisson of the Alfheim elves. And you are?"

The kelpie blinked. He looked around, then finally noticed Hrokr standing close enough to kiss. "Aye, lad, ye've got some strong concealments there, dinnae ye?" He sniffed again, and glanced away, as if he couldn't be bothered to continue their conversation.

"Hey! Wayne! Pay attention!" Hrokr snapped his fingers in front of the kelpie's face.

"I thought ye left," the kelpie said. "Mah name's not Wayne."

Ah, but the annoyance kept his attention. "Zander, then?"

The kelpie frowned. "Like I'd tell a Loki elf mah real name."

Kelpies did have their rules. Hrokr shrugged. "Well then, Travis, that's just too bad, now isn't it?"

The kelpie's eyes wandered out over the lake. "There be lasses here." He growled. "The Queen's pup is makin' mah life *hard*. Can't harm bitches." He took a step toward the water. "Must go home. Been commanded so."

So Hrokr had been correct; Ellie Jones had stolen the kelpie's bridle. Jones must have slapped some sort of "no murdering" order on him, which made sense. Hrokr would have done the same. The fewer lasses he tortured, the less likely it was that Alfheim's parental sheriff would make a ruckus by putting a silver bullet in his handsome skull. "Sucks to be you, Mason."

Though Hrokr would rather he stayed in Alfheim.

The kelpie snarled. "Mah name's not Mason."

"Sure thing, Kyle."

"What d'ye want, elf?" The kelpie gave Hrokr a little shove.

He did not move backward, or twist, or shift his center of gravity. He was an elf and this beautiful murdering fae was not worth the faintest twitch.

The kelpie frowned again.

A wave of magic burst through the trees and out over the water. The kelpie breathed it in, as did Hrokr, and they stood there for a long moment bathed in the fire of an overheating witch.

"Serves her right." The kelpie spat on the rocks. "Sad little custard."

Hrokr sighed. Kelpies were a chore. Their attitudes were as predictable as they were grating and this one was no different than the rest of his kind. Next he'd be spewing some dumb conspiracy theory about how red lipstick was invented specifically to harass his personal senses, or some nonsense about tidiness and crustacean gods.

Right now, Hrokr needed him to focus. "Frank Victorsson's *mean*, isn't he, Tyler?" So very untrusting and nasty, and so very in Hrokr's way. "Interfering like *that*."

If Frank wasn't going to help Hrokr hide from his grandfather, then Hrokr was going to take matters into his own hands.

"And?" the kelpie said.

"Brodie, Brodie, Brodie..." Hrokr pinched the bridge of his nose. "*Revenge*, you handsome numpty."

"Brodie?" The kelpie's face twisted up in confusion. "Ye're th' numpty, elf."

Hrokr looked up at the sky and sighed again. This kelpie was as thick as a Scottish castle wall. "Do you want your bridle back or not, Kylo?"

The kelpie dipped the toe of his boot into the lake. "I wanna drag that nettle-faced cragwanker under an' watch her gasp in th' deepest of the dark places. That'll get me mah bridle back."

"Yes, yes. Whatever." Hrokr would let the kelpie believe what he wanted as long as he stayed motivated. He slapped the kelpie's non-wounded shoulder. "Skylar, my new friend, we have work! There's someone I want you to find...."

II.

Alfheim Regional Hospital, Alfheim, Minnesota....

HIS WIFE HAD PROMISED their child to the World Raven.

Dagrun had needed to get free of St. Martin's magic. She'd had to placate a trickster. The elves needed to learn the truth about whose magic they were dealing with. The world was on the cusp of a new Ragnarok.

Arne understood why. Reasons and whys connected up in spectacular clarity in his mind.

He rubbed his notched ear. His wife had promised their child to a trickster.

He'd already known a Ragnarok approached. The world had its cycles. The new information Dagrun brought home was the intensity of the coming storm.

Most Ragnaroks hit like hurricanes. Some were category twos. Other, category fives. Involvement of World Spirits meant they were staring down the barrel of an extinction event.

And his wife had traded their unborn babe for help saving the world.

Arne stood at the window and rubbed his sore shoulder—the scuffle with Titania had left him with a twinge he'd need to massage out tonight, something he shouldn't have to do, with his magic. And as King.

His centuries were clearly catching up with him.

Dagrun flipped through a city file her office manager had brought over. His wife would continue serving the mundanes through the coming storm, and through giving birth if the healers would let her.

She tapped the paper. "The grant money came through."

She and Magnus had been working on establishing farm-to-table distribution from the neighboring tribal lands into the Farmer's Market and restaurants of Alfheim. They could have easily funded the entire project themselves, but securing federal-level grant money helped legitimize the project in the eyes of the wary local Tribal Councils.

Arne nodded. "Good."

Dagrun's head tilted to the side. She, like Arne, only partially glamoured while in her private hospital room. Most everyone who came in and out of the room understood that they were magicals, and knew to keep that information to themselves.

She'd been at his side for centuries, standing with him as the town grew, managing their interactions with the mundanes' rising technology, and running diplomacy with her father in Iceland. She was the backbone of Alfheim, not him.

A thousand years ago, his mother had stepped between Fenrir and her people. She saved the mundanes even as that Ragnarok caused cataclysmic damage to the elves and their gods.

This time, there were more mundanes to worry about, and more gods.

"The children will be all right," Dagrun said. "No matter what Raven wants." She closed her folder and set it aside.

He walked over and sat on the edge of her bed. She leaned forward and pressed her cheek against his shoulder. Arne Odinsson gently hugged his wife, careful of her mending ribs. At least this time, they had each other, promises to a trickster god notwithstanding.

A wave of power rolled through Alfheim. Both Arne and Dag—and all elves and wolves in Alfheim, he knew—turned toward the source: the woods around Frank's lake.

Hot power hit the hospital. Overheating, witch-born power.

They'd known they had a witch in Alfheim. She'd appeared the night after Frank's "brother" attacked Akeyla, but no one had been able to locate her, or to communicate, or to judge if she was a danger because there were concealments much like the ones he'd installed to keep his son from becoming a problem.

This witch likely supplied the flawless seer photographs that Frank lied about coming from that useless notebook, which meant she wasn't showing the psychosis that took Rose. And Frank was clearly in love with someone no one in town had met.

Arne understood how to work around concealments he could not influence. He trusted his gut, and his gut said that this witch was worth protecting.

Dagrun's eyes widened. "We have another witch?"

Arne wove his fingers and held up her hand. "Yes. Our new seer."

"Ah," she said, as she remembered that they could not remember anything beyond "seer."

Arne closed his eyes and tuned his ear into the wave. "Listen."

The wave slowed and cooled. It fluttered for a second, almost at a standstill, until the engine generating the concealments began to pull it back.

Dagrun's lips rounded. "Arne, that much power in Alfheim is not safe."

No, it wasn't. But they had an extinction-level Ragnarok coming. They could use all the help they could get.

And this witch wouldn't take their babe.

The wave changed.

What had been fae-born became steadfast and sturdy. It rooted to the earth and it reached for the sky. It knew all the cycles, old and new, and lived them intimately. And it touched all the realms.

Dagrun stared at the window. "By Odin, it's here, Arne. It came *here*," she breathed.

There was no stopping the Ragnarok now. No recourse.

Yggdrasil had come to witness the end of their world.

Arne kissed Dagrun's fingers. He refused to let the inevitable happen. He refused to allow World Spirits or Titania or that scum-sucking bloviator, Oberon, to harm his family. He would keep his wife and children safe.

No matter the cost.

III.

Oberon's Castle, the Fae Realms….

"WHY AM I HERE, ROBIN?" Wrenn Goodfellow watched her mentor smooth the lines of his well-tailored midnight-blue uniform. His fidgeting made her fidget too, and she found herself mimicking his flattening of pockets and checking of jacket buttons.

Neither of them enjoyed the crispness of Oberon's new dress requirements. Robin, being a freewheeling Seelie, would rather prance around nearly naked. Wrenn, being taller and stronger than most mundane and fae alike, had found comfort in modern high-performance athletic apparel. Two centuries of corsets and idiotic shoes had finally given way to stretchy, shimmering jackets, leggings, and butt-kicking boots.

"You are here—" Robin smoothed his luscious black curls away from his cute little horn nubs. They weren't always cute or little, but he tended to glamour more toward "sweet young man" than full Bacchus these days, "—because the dryads are back."

The intelligence dryads and naiads sent out to gather information after Samhain would trickle back in over the next few days. Two coming in early didn't mean anything.

Robin tossed her one of his prissy looks. He leaned close to her ear, still faux-shocked at her lack of enthusiasm. "I sent this pair into elf territory."

"What?" There were agreements. Nothing particularly binding—the elves were not stupid enough to make deals with the fae—but they did offer each other respect. No nosing around. No spying. General good neighbor stuff, which it seemed Robin had decided to ignore.

He could have gotten into real trouble if they'd been caught.

He waved his hand dismissively as if he'd take on any pain if it helped her get the information she needed.

Elves did not freely show their business, or their magicks, but she'd already gathered enough evidence that the North American enclave had harbored vampires—and that those vampires had likely bitten the elves on the ass. "Did that video of the little elf girl get Oberon to authorize sending in investigators?"

Robin screwed up his face in an expression that said *maybe, maybe not.*

"What does that mean?" she asked.

"It means," he ushered her into the antechamber of the dryad's reporting sanctum, "that the *why* in all this is above both our pay grades."

Robin Goodfellow had found her wandering in the forest outside Edinburgh the night she escaped her captor. Robin had never once asked for favors. He was now, and had always been, a gentleman.

When Oberon offered her a place in his court, she'd declared herself of Robin's band as her thank you.

Which meant she knew the access that came with the Goodfellow name. "Above our pay grade" did not often apply. She nodded and followed Robin across the shimmering red and green magic that was the gate into the dryads' sanctum.

Robin held his finger to his lips. One did not speak inside the sanctum. One only listened.

Two quick steps and they stood under the massive stones that made up the henge in which the dryads reported. The two intelligence agents in their antlered armor stood in the center. They mirrored each other's movements, as was their way, and sent their report into the curls of magic flowing through the sanctum like ghosts of an aurora.

They told of the elves' land, and a blizzard. Of how, with elves, the forest and its animals lived protected from the pollution and murder of the mundanes, and how the land understood that soon, not even its magicals could stop the coming death and damage.

Wrenn shook her head. Mundanes were destructive to the natural world.

The dryads continued: The land spoke of werewolves and elves and witches gone mad. Of concealments they could not read and of the wolves masquerading as genies.

Then they spoke of a vampire.

Dracula.

Wrenn shuddered as if she'd fallen under a frozen lake's ice. Only *parts* of Dracula existed anymore. Parts the man who had enslaved her had found.

It's him, she mouthed to Robin. She now had proof that he'd survived that night in Edinburgh—and evidence that he might still be out there terrorizing the world.

Robin touched his lips again, and leaned his head toward the dryads.

There was another, the dryads reported. A big man who was mundane, yet not. A man who heard the dryads, and saw their magic.

Robin squeezed her hand.

No, she thought. The vampire her captor had created was bad enough, but this man—this *monster*—was why he'd kidnapped her in the first place.

She had no memory of her life before she'd come to live in Edinburgh, but she knew that all the pain, all the imprisonment, all the abuse happened because her captor had promised the monster a bride.

Robin nodded once. He understood.

He pulled his phone out of his pocket. He tapped on the fae app he used to call up gateways, then turned it so she could see.

The closest gate to the elves' home was some distance north, situated on a trail inside protected land labeled Paul Bunyan State Forest.

Thank you, she mouthed.

Victor Frankenstein had held her captive. He'd unleashed a demigod of a vampire. And he'd lied about the death of his first mistake.

A mistake, like the vampires, harbored by elves.

Wrenn Goodfellow turned on her heels. She'd never, not once, made others pay for her pain and existence. The men of Frankenstein did.

So now she hunted monsters.

DEATH KISSED

W hen Wrenn Goodfellow comes looking to clean up Alfheim, it's up to Sheriff Ed Martinez to keep her away from not only Frank and the elves, but also the people he cares the most about —his family.

DEATH KISSED AVAILABLE NOW!

GET FREE BOOKS

SUBSCRIBE TO KRIS AUSTEN RADCLIFFE'S NEWSLETTER

You will be notified when Kris Austen Radcliffe's next novel is released, as well as gain access to an occasional free bit of author-produced goodness. Your email address will never be shared and you can unsubscribe at any time.

WWW.SIXTALONSIGN.COM/MAILING-LIST-SIGN-UP/

THE WORLDS OF
KRIS AUSTEN RADCLIFFE

Smart Urban Fantasy:

Northern Creatures

Monster Born

Vampire Cursed

Elf Raised

Wolf Hunted

Fae Touched

Death Kissed

God Forsaken

Magic Scorned

Witch Burned (*coming soon*)

Northern Creatures Box Set One: Books 1-3

Northern Creatures Box Set Two: Books 4-6

Genre-bending Science Fiction about
love, family, and dragons:

WORLD ON FIRE

Series one

Fate Fire Shifter Dragon

Games of Fate

Flux of Skin

Fifth of Blood

Bonds Broken & Silent

All But Human

Men and Beasts

The Burning World

Dragon's Fate and Other Stories

Series Two

Witch of the Midnight Blade: The Complete Series

Series Three

World on Fire

Call of the Dragonslayer (*coming soon*)

Hot Contemporary Romance:

The Quidell Brothers

Thomas's Muse

Daniel's Fire

Robert's Soul

Thomas's Need

Quidell Brothers Box Set

Includes:

Thomas's Muse

Daniel's Fire

Roberts's Soul

ABOUT THE AUTHOR

Kris's Science Fiction universe, **World on Fire**, brings her descriptive touch to the fantastic. Her Urban Fantasy series, **Northern Creatures**, sets her magic free. She's traversed many storytelling worlds including dabbles in film and comic books, spent time as a talent agent and a textbook photo coordinator, as well written nonfiction. But she craved narrative and richly-textured worlds—and unexpected, true love.

Kris lives in Minnesota with one husband, two daughters, and three cats.

For more information
www.krisaustenradcliffe.com

www.ingramcontent.com/pod-product-compliance
Lightning Source LLC
Chambersburg PA
CBHW071133200626
46817CB00018B/2939